THE MAD TRIST

The Comte de Saint-Germain has come into possession of a copy of *The Mad Trist*, the book from which
Edgar Allan Poe and Roderick Usher read aloud before the collapse recorded in "The Fall of the House
of Usher." The Comte wants to make a present of it
to detective Auguste Dupin, but Dupin's faithful companion is *en route* for England, and cannot deliver the
volume immediately.

In any case, he is certain that his friend, Richard
Carstairs, will be just as interested in reading the
supposedly accursed volume as he is. Despite the warn-
ings issued by a rival bibliophile, Stephen Coningsby,
Dupin's friend is unintimidated by the prospect of
reading a forbidden book. After all, Dupin has a whole
shelf full of them, and has never sustained any harm
therefrom...!

A classic tale of horror.

Borgo Press Fiction by BRIAN STABLEFORD

THE MAD TRIST

A ROMANCE OF BIBLIOMANIA

BRIAN STABLEFORD

THE BORGO PRESS

MMX

THE MAD TRIST

FIRST EDITION

Published by Wildside Press LLC

www.wildsidebooks.com

DEDICATION

For Cymantha,

Twenty Years On

CONTENTS

"And now, the champion, having escaped from the terrible fury of the dragon, bethinking himself of the golden shield, and of the breaking up of the enchantment which was upon it, removed the carcass from out of the way before him, and approached valorously over the silver pavement of the castle to where the shield was upon the wall; which in sooth tarried not for his full coming, but fell down at his feet upon the silver floor, with a mighty great and terrible ringing sound."

Sir Launcelot Canning, *The Mad Trist* (allegedly *circa* 1450)

"Voluptuousness is a strong beast, and has many instruments to draw to Lust; but men are so forward of themselves thereto, as they need none to hail them."

Jane Anger, *Her Protection for Women* (1589)

"'We have put her living in the tomb! Said I not that my senses were acute? I *now* tell you that I heard her first feeble movements in the hollow coffin. I heard them, many, many says ago, yet I dared not, I dared not speak! And now—tonight—Ethelred—ha! ha!—the breaking of the hermit's door, and the death-cry of the dragon, and the clangor of the shield,—say, rather, the rending of her coffin, and the grating of the iron hinges of her prison, and her struggles within the archway of the vault! Oh! whither shall I fly? Will she not be here anon? Is she not hurrying to upbraid me for my haste? Have I not heard her footstep on the stair? Do I not distinguish that heavy and horrible beating of her heart? Madman!'—here he sprang furiously to his feet, and shrieked out his syllables, as if in the effort he were giving up his soul—'Madman! I tell you that she now stands without the door.'"

Edgar Poe, "The Fall of the House of Usher" (1839)

CHAPTER ONE
An Unexpected Gift

The coachman was struggling to load my trunk on to his cab, in order that I might set off for the *Messageries générales*, having reserved a seat on the diligence to Boulogne, when I heard a voice behind me, calling my name. Although I was in something of a hurry, fearful of missing the coach if the traffic proved to be bad or there was any dawdling, I could not help looking around.

The man hurrying toward me, twirling his cane as if it were a paddle-wheel assisting his progress, was known to me only by his pseudonym, the Comte de Saint-Germain. He was the President of the Philosophical Harmonic Society of Paris, an organization of esoteric mesmerists. I had only met him on two or three occasions, always in the company of my friend Auguste Dupin—who regarded him as a charlatan and a villain, although I had nothing in particular against him myself. To tell the truth, I had previously found him rather charming and amusing, although that did not make his appearance any the less unwelcome at that particular moment.

I greeted him with a slight bow. "I'm sorry, Saint-Germain," I said, "but I can't stop to chat with you or anyone else. I'm bound for England, and if I miss this morning's diligence, I'll miss my ferry too."

He seemed slightly offended by my abruptness, although my tone had not been surly. "Then I'm very glad to have caught you before you left," he said. "I'd like to ask you a favor, if

I may—and to be honest, I feel that you owe me one. Dupin might disagree, I know, but he's an unreasonable chap at the best of times, and he really ought to admit that I helped the two of you out of a bit of a hole back in February."

"How is Mademoiselle Valdemar?" I asked, reflexively.

"On the mend, I think—poor darling. Dupin really gave her a scare, you know. I suppose he couldn't have known how hard she'd be hit by his little charade, but he could have been a little gentler and still won the day. She's only a woman, after all."

"What do you want, Saint-Germain?" I asked him, glancing sideways at the coachman, who seemed to be making heavy weather of his task.

The mesmerist followed my glance, and immediately stepped forward to help. He was a tall man, reasonably well-built, and the two of them had the trunk securely stowed in no time. Oddly enough, I felt slightly annoyed by his intervention, as if it were a criticism aimed at my own reluctance to lend assistance. I was still feeling the twinges in my back that had resulted from dragging the trunk outside, though, and I had every intention of giving the coachman a reasonable *pourboire*, provided that I got to the *Messageries* in time.

"I want to repair my relationship with Dupin," Saint-Germain said, a trifle belatedly, in answer to my query. "I see no need at all for the enmity that seems to have grown up between us, and I feel bad about my part in it. It all blew up in the first place, you know, because of a silly quarrel over a book. You're a collector yourself, in a small way, so you know how these things go. We both wanted the volume in question; I procured it. He might imagine that I behaved underhandedly, but the simple fact is that I paid the asking price, and bought it fair and square. Anyhow, I'm willing to make amends. I recently came across a volume that he's been after for years, and I'd like to make him a present of it, as a peace offering. It's not my sort of thing, to be honest—an old romance, printed in English—and I'm not the kind of man to hoard a book in my library simply because it's rare. He wants it far more than I do, so the gentlemanly thing to do is to let him have it."

"Without asking anything in return?" I said, skeptically.

"Not a thing," he replied. "Of course, if this small gesture, coupled with the favor I did him in February, were finally to persuade him that we might be friends, he might feel that it would be a nice gesture to reciprocate in kind—but I wouldn't dream of asking for a formal *quid pro quo*. This is a gift, and nothing more." He tapped his jacket pocket as he pronounced the last sentence. I had noticed that the garment was not hanging properly, and had wondered what had persuaded him to compromise the dandy's code. The bulge was not very large, and I concluded that the volume was a small octavo, and rather slim.

"I can't deliver it to him," I said. "As I told you, I'm bound for England, and won't be back for a fortnight, at least. You'll have to take it to Dupin's apartment yourself."

"But I've just come from there. That old witch of a concierge has strict orders not to let me in, it seems, or even to convey a message on my behalf. I could have entrusted the book to her, I suppose, but I really couldn't trust her not to throw it on the rubbish-heap, without even letting her master know. You, I can trust. You know what books are worth, to collectors and to scholars. You might even be interested in reading it yourself, given that it's printed in your native tongue. Its prose is turgid, but it has a certain antiquarian interest."

"What is it?" I asked, unable to resist the dire temptation of curiosity.

"Sir Launcelot Canning's *The Mad Trist*. The one and only printed edition, issued from St. Paul's Churchyard in Tudor times. The manuscript is said to be lost, and rumor has it that less than a dozen copies of the printed version survived the hangman's bonfire—although I can't see any earthly reason why it should have been banned by Whitgift's carrion crows, as there's nothing remotely seditious or irreligious in it"

I had pricked up my ears at the mention of the title, but I had contrived to maintain my attitude without giving any evident sign of my interest. I had heard of *The Mad Trist*, by virtue of the references made to it in one of my American correspondent's most famous tales. To be sure, the tale had not attributed any significant literary interest to Canning's romance, but the mere fact of the book's mention was significant to me. Poe had read it—or part of it, at least—in the home of his old friend Roderick Usher, who had been tragically killed when his house had collapsed, fatally undermined by the waters of the stagnant tarn on whose shore it stood. Poe had added some fine Gothic flourishes to the tale, as he invariably did when adapting episodes of his quotidian life to his literary purposes.

I had not known that Dupin was eager to find a copy of the book in question. He had never mentioned it to me, even after I had given him a copy of "The Fall of the House of Usher", but he had presumably mentioned the title to Père France and the other booksellers whose shops he frequented. Booksellers are notoriously garrulous; it was not at all surprising that a rival collector should be better informed than I was on such a score.

I was, in any case, on my way to visit an old friend of my own, who was an aficionado of rare books himself, and whose house likewise stood on the shore of a little lake—although I hoped to find the dwelling in question in far better condition than Poe had found Roderick Usher's house, and I remembered the lake as a bright and charming location. I thought that it might be amusing, if not apposite, were the two of us to sit together one evening and read the text aloud, as Poe and Roderick Usher had…without, of course, finding any echo of the text in the aftermath of a premature burial. So far as I knew, both my friend's sisters were in the best of health, and he certainly had no family vault in his cellar.

"Very well," I said to Saint-Germain, as I prepared to climb into the coach. "I'll take it off your hands—so long as you accept that I won't be able to pass it on to Dupin for at least a fortnight."

I half-expected him to object that it would only take me a few moments to deposit it in my house, but he seemed relieved that I had agreed to take it at all. "That's all right," the mesmerist assured me. "I know that you'll take good care of it in the interim—you're a connoisseur yourself, after all." So saying, he took the little volume out of his pocket, and handed it over to me before I closed the carriage door. It was shabbily bound in the worst black leather I had ever encountered, and had not been a handsome or well-made book when its pages were fresh off the press, but it was intact and seemingly readable.

I put it in my own pocket after the merest glance; I was in a hurry, after all.

"At least my coat hangs properly now," Saint-Germain observed, still peering at me through the *portière*. "I hate asymmetry—but it's rumoured that even Lord Byron kept a book in his pocket more often than not, and he was the true father of dandyism, not Brummell. By all accounts, Brummell was a donkey, and no man lacking in intellect could possibly make himself into a true and worthy work of art—don't you agree?"

I might have agreed that, so far as I had heard, Beau Brummell really had been a man of limited intelligence, but it seemed a trifle unfair to slander a dead man, and I was in too much of a hurry to care about the theory and practise of dandyism, even as it was flatteringly reflected in the career of Lord Byron or the works of Honoré de Balzac. "Thank you, Saint-Germain," I said, hurriedly, while the coachman was pausing to allow us to complete our conversation. "I'll put in a good word for you when I give it to Dupin, but I can't guarantee that it will alter his opinion."

"We can but try," said Saint-Germain, "and make sure that we have done all that we can to make things right. My conscience is clear now, and I thank you for that."

"You're welcome," I told him—but I must confess that I was rather glad when the coachman responded immediately to the impact of the knob of my stick on the casing of the vehicle, and urged his horse to action. I looked back through the *portière* to see Saint-Germain stride away, heading westwards into the district whose name he had appropriated, in imitation of a notorious impostor of the previous century.

As I looked back, however, I also noticed a second man,

thinner and shabbier in appearance, who appeared to be watching Saint-Germain as the latter moved off. I saw the thin man turn abruptly as Saint-German drew away, and leap into another fiacre, giving the coachman a hasty instruction as he did so.

It was not at all surprising that the other fiacre should head for the Pont Neuf, as my own vehicle was doing—but I kept glancing back continually, once we had crossed the river, and invariably saw it behind me. I could not shake off the conviction that it was following my own cab, and although I tried to reassure myself that, even if it ended up at the *Messageries*, there would be no cause for amazement or alarm, I found myself wishing at every crossroads that it would turn aside and head for some other destination.

The further the two fiacres went, however, the more obvious it seemed that the second was deliberately dogging the steps of the first. I considered the possibility of asking my coachman to speed up, or even acquainting him with my anxieties and imploring him to take evasive action, but decided that either request would be futile. His nag was already doing its poor best, and the traffic conditions would not have permitted the animal to go faster, or maneuver more cleverly, even if it had been the finest post-horse in the capital.

Mercifully, the coachman did not have to get my trunk down when we reached the *Messageries*, or load it on to the waiting diligence; there were eager porters waiting to attend to that, while I paid him off and went into the office to present the receipt for my reservation.

When I came out of the office again, however, intending to take my seat immediately—and, in truth, there was no time to waste before the appointed moment of departure—I found the thin man who had followed me waiting on the forecourt. Unlike Saint-Germain, he was certainly no dandy, being dressed in a conspicuously worn and outdated jacket and riding breeches that seemed to have gone hunting at least once too often. His boots were spattered with dried mud, although the weather was fine and there had been no rain in Paris for three days. I was relieved to observe, now that I could do so at close range, that he was at least ten years older than me, and that his slenderness was more reminiscent of emaciation than a wiry athleticism. His sallow complexion did not advertise a vigorous constitution.

"Whatever you paid Saint-Germain for that book," the stranger said, forthrightly, "I'll double it." He spoke in French but his accent immediately revealed him to be English, so I replied in my native language.

"The calculation would be futile, sir," I said, injecting as much contempt into my tone as I could, "for I did not pay him anything." I moved as if to go around him and head for the diligence, but he moved to block my path, very rudely. I was not quite ready to shove him out of the way, as yet, so I paused again.

"So much the better," he said, gruffly, in English. "Name your price, in francs or guineas, as you please." I took offense at his tone, although I was not so preoccupied with my own frustration to neglect the skills I had learned from Dupin. I noted that the revelation that Saint-Germain had demanded no payment for the book seemed to have surprised him—and perhaps even disturbed him.

"The book is not mine to sell, sir," I told him, intemperately, "but even if it were, I would not sell it to you for all the gold you might have about your person, and twice as much again. Now stand aside, for I have to take my seat in the coach."

He glanced behind, but did not move. "That coach?" he said, as if noticing it for the first time. "But that's not bound for Le Havre—it's the diligence to Boulogne."

"Full marks for observation," I said, sarcastically, wondering why his sallow complexion had turned a little paler. "Now, get out of my way, or I shall be forced to knock you down."

He seemed to pull himself together then, and regret his rudeness. "I'm sorry," he said, "but if you will not let me take the book, you must not take it to England. Even in America, it would not be entirely safe, but you *must not* take it to England.

Do you have the slightest idea what you have in your custody?"

"I have not the slightest idea who *you* are," I pointed out, "save for the fact that you're an English boor of the worst sort. This is your third warning—next time, I strike."

I am not an unduly athletic man, but I am not small, and can seem intimidating in confrontation with men of his meager sort. Besides, he had no stick and I was equipped with the stoutest one I owned, in anticipation of some serious walking in the wilds of Essex.

The boor did step aside, but as I hurried past him, heading for the diligence like an arrow, he turned and did his level best to keep pace with me. Because I was unwilling to lower myself actually to breaking into a run—a reluctance that he did not share—he was able to keep up, but I only had some thirty meters to cover, and he obviously realized that he only had seconds to make his point. He stammered further apologies and groped in his pocket, eventually fetching out a soiled visiting card, which he thrust at me insistently.

Politeness engraves deep habits, so I took it automatically, but I did not glance at it. As I set my boot-heel on the footplate in order to haul myself up into the coach, my pursuer turned his attention to the postillion, demanding how much a seat would cost. The postillion did not bother to instruct him as to the correct procedure for obtaining a reservation, but simply told him, brutally, that every place was taken, even on the *impériale*.

"Saint-Germain has tricked you!" he shouted at me, as I took my seat. The other passengers looked at me curiously, but I simply shrugged my shoulders, as if to say that he was evidently a madman, and that his behaviour was no responsibility of mine.

Mercifully, there was no one else to board the vehicle, and as soon as the coachman and postillion had taken their positions, it moved off. The four horses entrusted with its traction were finer by far than the hack that had bought me across the river. Within two minutes, the *Messageries* was two hundred meters behind us, and I felt safe—but the last thing that the madman had shouted was still ringing in my ears.

"Whatever occurs, and however fascinated you become," the poor fellow had howled, *"don't read the final chapter!"*

CHAPTER TWO
Aboard the Diligence

I was so determined to remain calm and dignified that I waited until we had passed Pontoise to open my clenched fist and look at the card that I had taken.

The name engraved on it was Stephen Coningsby, and instead of a profession, it bore the single word: *Bibliomaniac*.

A truer word was never writ, I thought. *Thank God he does not know who I am*. The address on the card was in Hackney, which I knew to be on the eastern border of London's conurbation.

My gratitude regarding Mr. Coningsby's ignorance was short-lived, when I realized that he only had to go into the office of the *Messageries*, and inquire in a sufficiently cunning manner—or part with a minimal bribe—to find out what was recorded in their ledger: not merely my name but my Paris address. It seemed inconceivable that the information in question would do him much good, though, and I could not imagine that he would go so far as to track me down in England, even if that were possible, in the hope of retrieving the book that Saint-Germain had entrusted to me. I decided to put him out of my mind and give him no further thought, lest the memory of our meeting cast a shadow over my reunion with my old friend.

That was easier to think than to do, however, and I had to postpone the mental operation, at least for a while. What had Coningsby meant, I could not help but wonder, by saying that Saint-German had tricked me? How could he have tricked

me—and why? It seemed, on due reflection, that the only significance that could possibly be attached to the allegation was that
Saint-Germain had not meant the book for Dupin at all, but for
me, and that he had timed its delivery to make certain that I
would have no alternative, if I accepted it at all, but to take it to
England with me. But what concern of Coningsby's could that
possibly be? Why on Earth would Saint-German want the book
taken to England, and why, if he did, would he not have taken
it himself, or entrusted it to one of his acolytes in the Harmonic
Society? Even if Dupin were correct in his estimation of Saint-
Germain, and the latter really was a thoroughly bad man, what
could he possibly gain by making me the custodian of a book?

I had, of course, heard of "forbidden books"—Dupin had a
veritable collection of them, including a copy of the *Harmonies
de l'enfer* that was said to be as dangerous as it was priceless—
but there was no indication in Poe's story of "The Fall of the
House of Usher" that *The Mad Trist* was anything but a dull
mock-Medieval romance, of no particular value outside its rarity.
Thanks to my acquaintance with Dupin, I could cite the titles of
several books that were said to carry nasty curses, and at least
two that were rumored to be fatal to anyone who read them all
the way through, but I had never placed the slightest credence
in such tales, and I could not believe that Saint-Germain would
credit them either. He was, after all, a fake and a poseur, who
did not even try to maintain his pretence when he was in the
company of men like Dupin, who were immune to such foolery.
Dupin had suggested to me that the false mage might well have
fallen for his own publicity to some extent, since becoming
President of the Harmonic Society, but that could hardly have
overwhelmed him with a universal credulity.

Retreating into my corner, and ignoring the discussion that
two of my neighbors had struck up, in strident English, regarding
Robert Peel's credentials as a statesman, and whether the Tory
party would fall apart if he went ahead with his proposed repeal
of the corn laws, I took out *The Mad Trist* and opened it to the
title page.

The lettering on the page was artfully surrounded by a figurative illustration depicting a knight in armor—presumably Ethelred, the story's protagonist—in conflict with a snaky dragon, whose coils wound around both title and author's name. The engraving was blurred and smudged, though, and the whole page badly foxed. At the bottom was an inscription declaring the text to have been printed by "the Widow Orwin" on behalf of "J.B." at the sign of the Black Bear in St. Paul's Churchyard, in the year 1593.

The caption was slightly surprising, in that there could not have been very many female printers active in St. Paul's Churchyard in Tudor England, but I knew enough about history to be well aware that women of that era could own property in their own right, and even operate businesses, if they acquired them by inheritance. Presumably, the widow Orwin's husband had been a printer, and she had inherited his press along with his other goods and chattels. The fact that England had been ruled at the time by Queen Elizabeth—whose hegemony had been triumphantly secured by the defeat of the Spanish Armada, five years before *The Mad Trist* had been printed—had doubtless assisted the status of women in London, at least temporarily.

The book had no preface, but it did carry a note on the reverse of the title-page advertising the fact that the text had been composed "circa 1450" by "a gentile night" (*sic*) and that it had never been printed before, this edition having been taken direct from "the onlye manuscript". I was not unduly surprised that a sixteenth-century typesetter could render "manuscript" correctly while making an obvious mistake, even by the loose standards of Tudor spelling, in rendering the word "knight" and also substituting "gentile"—which was used at that time as a synonym of "heathen"—for "genteel".

I was tempted to turn to the text then—indeed, I was tempted to turn directly to the final chapter, and read it forthwith—but I knew that reading the end before the beginning would spoil whatever pleasure the text was capable of giving, and the volume's lack of bulk suggested that I would be able to read the whole story in a couple of hours if I did so silently, and little more than four if I were to read it aloud. In any case, it seemed somehow unsporting and disrespectful to take such a liberty. Given that the volume was held to be precious, and that it occupied such an important place in what many people considered to be my American correspondent's finest tale, I felt that I ought to do it full justice, and wait for an interval of tranquility before I began it—even if that meant postponing the pleasure until I was safely in Essex, at the home of my old friend Richard Carstairs. Carstairs would, I supposed, be interested to read it himself, or hear it read aloud.

Indeed, I could easily imagine myself sitting beside the hearth in the drawing-room of the quaintly-named Burnt Oak Lodge, reading *The Mad Trist* aloud, not merely to Richard but to his younger sisters, Imogen and Esmeralda, whom I had not seen for three years, when even the older of the two had been little more than a child. I had read to the two girls last time I had visited the Lodge, from a book of Gothic tales featuring witches, curses and ghosts—a pastime that they had enjoyed as much as I had, although Richard had had obvious reservations as to whether such lurid material was really suitable for Imogen, let alone Esmeralda. The girls themselves had, however, revelled in the tales, and had seemed very grateful to me for helping to open a breach in their elder brother's censorious strictness— an overprotective attitude doubtless originating in an exaggerated awareness of the fact that he was acting *in loco parentis*, following the deaths of his father and his mother, two years apart but both in high summer, of a disease known locally as "marsh fever".

Instead of consulting Sir Launcelot Canning's text, I deliberately turned back to the fly-leaf positioned ahead of the title-page. That too was foxed, and somewhat soiled, but something had been written on it by a former custodian of the volume. The appalling quality of the ink that had been used, and the inexpert manner in which the goose-quill had been plied, made the scrawl all-but-illegible, but I thought that it read: "Jane Anger, her boke."

Oddly enough, the name of "Jane Anger" was not unfamiliar to me, although I knew that the name had been used as a mere pseudonym in the context in which I had encountered it. My own one-time interest in English Romantic poetry, especially that of what Robert Southey had called "the Satanic school"— consisting primarily of works by Byron and Shelley—had led me to take a passing interest in Shelley's widow, Mary, and thus in her mother, Mary Wollstonecraft. Mary Wollstonecraft had spent a great deal of time in Paris in the epoch of the Revolution of 1789, and was still fondly remembered there by old Jacobins and by society ladies besotted with her *Vindication of the Rights of Women*. It was while I was chatting to one of those redoubtable ladies about the elder Mary, at one of the rare social events I attended, that she had asked me whether I knew of the great pioneer of English protest in regard to women's rights, Jane Anger. When I had confessed ignorance, the lady in question had undertaken to enlighten me, at least to the limited extent of her own knowledge. Apparently, "Jane Anger" had been a contemporary of Elizabeth Tudor, who had produced a tract entitled *Her Protection for Women* in response to a scurrilous misogynistic pamphlet entitled *His Surfeit in Love*, but had been forced to hide her true identity behind a *nom de guerre* for fear of reprisals.

I wondered, briefly, whether the one-time owner of *The Mad Trist* might have been the same Jane Anger, but I knew that "Anger" was an authentic English surname, and that Jane was the commonest of all English female Christian names, so it seemed more likely that the person who had scrawled the claim of ownership had been a different individual.

"Excuse me, sir," said one of my fellow passengers in French, as these thoughts drifted through my mind, "but might I know the title of the book that you are holding so tenderly?"

The speaker was a woman. The person in the corner seat opposite my own was one of the gentlemen obsessed with Peel and the corn laws—a topic that he was discussing fervently with my neighbor to the right—but the lady did not appear to be traveling with him…or, indeed, with anyone, even a maid. She was between thirty and forty years of age, and her traveling costume, though utterly conventional, seemed to be well-tailored. Her bonnet was plain, but not cheap, and the blonde hair tucked within it was neatly arranged. Her blue eyes, set within a handsome face, were simultaneously frank and piercing.

When I hesitated to answer, the lady held up the book that she was holding in her own delicate hands; it was Victor Hugo's *Notre-Dame de Paris*. "Forgive me," she said, "but I'm merely a bibliophile, comparing notes. The road is good, I admit, but even the finest of public coaches is still a public coach, and I am subject to enough lurching and jolting to make reading difficult—more difficult than conversation, at any rate."

As she spoke, the Peel enthusiasts raised their baritone voices as if to drown out her gentle soprano, but that only made me more determined to accept the challenge. I told her the title of the book, and informed her as to my name.

"I am Madame Poyet," she informed me, but quickly added: "My English is not very good, I fear. What is the meaning of *trist*?" She pronounced it in a suitably guttural fashion, in order to differentiate it from *triste*.

"It means much the same as *rendezvous*," I told her. "Nowadays, the word is spelled t-r-y-s-t, but this is an old book, and Elizabethan spelling was a trifle haphazard. The word can also refer to a betrothal."

"But in your book, it refers to a *rendezvous?*"

It occurred to me, as she asked the question, that I was not entirely sure. I knew from reading Poe, of course, that the story involved the adventures and ordeals undergone by the hero, Ethelred, in trying to reach an appointed meeting with a lady, but I did not know whether or not she was his intended bride.

"Perhaps both," I replied, "but I shall not know exactly what the implication is until I reach the final chapter."

"Which the crazy man at the *Messageries* instructed you sternly you not to do," she said, laughing.

"Indeed," I said, echoing her laughter.

One of the Peel enthusiasts looked daggers at me, evidently feeling that I had no right to confuse an important political discussion in the Queen's English with mere merry chitchat in what he doubtless suspected to be neo-Jacobin French. He must, after all, have gathered that I was an American, and hence a Republican.

"And why is the trist mad?" Madame Poyet asked.

"Again, I don't know—perhaps because the author considers all amorous trysts to be mad. Love is often seen as a kind of madness, is it not? Our present infatuation with the emotion in question is a modern phenomenon; in previous eras, spontaneous passion was considered as something dubious, if not outrightly evil: a dire threat to social order, potentially disruptive of marriages made for diplomatic and economic purposes. Think of such tragic tales as those of Tristan and Yseult, or Abelard and Heloïse."

She held up her own book and said: "Or Claude Frollo and Esmeralda."

"In a manner of speaking—although they never enjoy a tryst. I don't want to spoil the ending for you, if you have not read the book before, but the only tryst that Esmeralda achieves, in the end, is most certainly a mad one."

"I know that I should have read it before," she said, as if my words had implied some criticism, "but I fear that I had neglected Monsieur Hugo's prose, while being very fond of his poetry. I fear that I have been a little late in being converted to the merits of the *roman*, whose classic examples have always seemed a little intimidating by virtue of their length; I have only recently discovered the joy of utter immersion in a story in which one seems to become a participant rather than a mere listener. George Sand worked the trick for me—I adore *Consuelo*—although I should also credit Monsieur de Vigny, love of whose epic *Éloa* persuaded me to read his *Cinq-Mars*."

"A very different work!" I said, laughing.

"Indeed," she replied. "Is Esmeralda doomed? I am already

beginning to fear that she might be."

"I really ought not to say," I riposted. "You must wait and see—that is the only honest way to deal with any text, especially a masterpiece."

She nodded in ready acquiescence. "It's impertinent of me, I know," she said, smiling warmly and arching her eyebrows in what I can only describe as a coquettish manner, "but I'm burning with curiosity. Why did the man at the *Messageries* shout after you like that? What on Earth did he mean?"

"I have no idea," I assured her. "The book was given to me by a man who is reputed to be a wizard, but he's an impostor, and quite harmless. I do not believe that it can be cursed, or that it can curse anyone who reads it."

"I've heard of books that can," she said.

"All readers have heard of books that can," I told her. "They read about them in other books, which have a vested interest in suggesting that books in general might have more power than they really do. Not that I wish to diminish the power that they really do have, for a book like the one you are holding really can change the way that people see the world—and Victor Hugo is not unduly modest in making that claim within the text, where he first compares the actual Notre-Dame de Paris to a book of history made in stone for people who cannot read, and then slyly implies that his own *Notre-Dame de Paris* is a similarly-layered edifice summarizing the soul of Paris, if not the collective soul of humankind."

I was proud of that little speech, which seemed to me to be one of the cleverest I had ever made, as well as one of the most elegant. I was beset by a urge to impress the lady, and felt that I was acquitting myself well. I regretted the fact that Dupin was not there to hear me, as he had had very few opportunities to see me play the gallant.

"I approve of the recent restoration," Madame Poyet told me, as if confiding a secret. "It makes the cathedral look so old, and so unruly."

"There is a Gothic revival in full swing throughout Europe,"

I told her. "It is the dark half of the Romantic Movement. You're too young to remember the novels of Mrs. Radcliffe, and if your English is less than fluent, you will not yet have had the opportunity to read the work of my good friend Edgar Poe, but you must have read Gautier's 'Morte amoureuse'."

"Oh yes!" she said. "I love tales of vampires, ghosts and witchcraft."

"Utter poppycock!" said the man next to me, loudly. It took me a moment or two to realize that he was no longer talking about the English corn laws, but had actually taken it upon himself to intrude upon our conversation.

"I beg your pardon?" I said, in English.

"So you should," he retorted. "Not fit subjects for discussion in a public coach, vampires, ghosts and witchcraft. Indecent idiocies, which should have been consigned to oblivion when the Age of Reason dawned. Now that Victoria's on the throne instead of the wretched Georges, all that Gothic nonsense has been consigned to oblivion in England, thankfully—and the memory of that rascal Byron with it. If the French had a stronger monarch, instead of that imbecile with the umbrella, the nation would have more intellectual backbone and all this nonsense about the *juste milieu* would be cast aside. This country is heading for another Revolution, you mark my words."

While grudgingly admiring the way he had maneuvered the topic of conversation back to his own political interests, from an apparently unpromising start, I still thought the Englishman's interruption intolerably rude. On Madame Poyet's behalf, I resented the insult to Louis-Philippe, although I had no great admiration for the man myself.

"The lady and I were discussing literature," I told Mr. Coningsby's compatriot, stiffly, "not stating our beliefs. Not that it would be any business of yours if we were wholehearted believers in magic, affiliated to some neo-Rosicrucian Lodge—but the fact is that we are rational, intelligent people who merely happen to have an aesthetic interest in what Alexander Baumgarten would call *heterocosmic creativity*."

I knew that he would not have the faintest idea who Alexander Baumgarten was, or what "heterocosmic creativity" might mean, but I also knew that he would not dare to admit it. As I had hoped, he limited his reply to a contemptuous snort. I did not like the way he looked at Madame Poyet, which was suggestive of the fact that he did not think a woman—especially a French woman—to be worthy of categorization as a person, let alone a rational and intelligent one. He had, however, succeeded in his objective, and spoiled our conversation.

Madame Poyet retreated into the pages of *Notre-Dame de Paris*, apparently resigned to suffering the jolts and lurches of the diligence, while I sat there seething, trying not to hear the resumed conversation about Peel and the Tories, let alone attend to its vapid arguments and counter-arguments.

CHAPTER THREE
The English Shore

I do not know why it is that coach-travel is so tiring, given that all one has to do is sit down and exercise patience, but by the time the diligence made its overnight stop in Caen I was exhausted. So was Madame Poyet, who retreated to her room as soon as we had finished supper—a meal that effortlessly lived down to the appalling reputation that food served in coaching inns, even in France, has nowadays acquired. I felt sore as well as tired, even though the journey had been as smooth as I had any right to expect, but I did not have bad dreams—not, at least, in the sense that they were nightmarish. Modesty forbids me to go into detail, but I have to confess, for the sake of the story I am telling, that Madame Poyet featured extensively within them.

I have described Madame Poyct as a handsome woman, and so she was, but Paris is full of handsome women, and I was usually more-or-less indifferent to their charms. I am not a misogynist, by any means, but I am by nature a self-contained person, who is not in the least discomfited by solitude and is perfectly happy when absorbed in a book, of almost any sort. Although I did not consider myself to be what is sometimes called "a confirmed bachelor", I had never felt any particular attraction to the prospect of marriage, even for money. In brief, I had never been "in love", and had never felt any particular desire to be. Had I felt any such desire, of course, I would have had the decency and common sense to turn my attention to an eligible spinster—I would never, under any circumstances, have allowed myself to entertain amorous designs on a married woman. Such designs are said to be very common in France, particularly in Paris—Balzac's *Comédie humaine* regards them as perfectly conventional—but I had retained my Bostonian standards throughout my long exile, and I do not think that the supposed gentleman who had boasted of the moral rearmament that had followed Queen Victoria's ascension to the English throne could possibly have had any advantage over me in terms of rectitude.

Having said all that, though, a man cannot help his dreams, and a man who is not a eunuch is bound to have dreams in which lust plays a mischievous part. The fact that I dreamed about Madame Poyet, however, did not have the slightest effect on my waking attitude to her, which remained utterly respectful.

Inevitably, it eventually turned out that the two Englishmen were booked on the same packet-boat as myself—but so was Madame Poyet, and a Cross-Channel ferry, mercifully, is much more spacious than a diligence. The weather remained mild, and *la Manche* was as smooth as I had ever seen it, so I was able to find the lady in a quiet corner of the deck, still immersed in the dire exploits of the hallucinated Claude Frollo and the luckless Esmeralda. As soon as I sat down beside her, however, she closed the book and immediately joined in with my hymn of complaint against the two English so-called gentlemen and their appalling crassness.

Mutual scorn inevitably creates a bond, and she was soon telling me what a wrench it had been to leave her two young daughters in Paris while she went to join her husband at Mivart's Hotel in London, but how necessary it was, since Monsieur Poyet had "business" to do, and because "business" was becoming more like diplomacy with every passing year, necessitating all manner of social interaction, for which a wife was sometimes indispensable.

"And a beautiful wife a great asset, I imagine," I told her, delighted to see her blush at the compliment and flutter her eyelashes.

In my turn, I explained that I was travelling to Burnt Oak

Lodge, not far from Pitsea, in Essex, to visit my old friend Richard Carstairs and his two sisters.

"What an odd name for a house," she observed.

"A deceptive one in more ways than one, alas," I told her. "It is not a lodge, as such—the equivalent French term would be *pavillon*—but a small manor house, whose dependencies have long disappeared. Local folklore claims that it is built on a site where an oak tree once stood, to whose trunk a witch was tied in order to be burned alive, but the legend is obviously false, since convicted witches were hanged in England, not burned— as were those in Salem, not so very far from my own home town."

I knew that she would like the tale, for she had already confessed her liking for such subject-matter. "Perhaps the witch was hanged from the boughs of the oak," she suggested, "and the tree was burned thereafter."

"It's possible," I conceded. "The house stands on a shallow ridge with a small lake on the landward side, however. If any witch were ever subjected to ill-treatment there, she'd more likely have been ducked in the water—it was a popular test at one time, though somewhat perverse, since the accused could only prove her innocence by drowning, and survival of the ordeal was bound to condemn her. I say *her*, of course, because most accused witches were women, often widows, reflecting the misogyny of the era....the sixteenth and seventeenth centuries, that is."

I became conscious that I was rambling on, and resolved to rein myself in—but I could not help being slightly stirred by Madame Poyet's presence. She *was* a beautiful woman, albeit a married one...and a man cannot help his instincts, no matter how determined he is in reserving his lustful impulses for appropriate objectives.

"Perhaps" she suggested, stubbornly, "the witch of the lodge was ducked first, and then—having survived that ordeal—was summarily hung from the nearest convenient tree...which might then have been burned, deliberately or accidentally."

I laughed. "If it pleases you to think so," I said.

She looked at me with her lovely blue eyes. "I have an instinct for these things," she assured me. "I have something of a gift—which, in the era we are talking about, might well have been taken for evidence of witchcraft. Mercifully, we are living in the nineteenth century, and I'm a respectable married woman, not a widow…as yet. But tell me more about your friend. If he is English and you are an American living in Paris, how do you know him?"

"I met him on the ship that carried me away from America, some ten years ago. My friendship with Edgar Poe had fired me with an enthusiasm for Romantic poetry, and Carstairs shared that enthusiasm to some extent, although he is primarily an antiquarian, interested in the Elizabethan period. He identifies the emotional and imagistic roots of modern Romanticism in the court poetry of the Elizabethan era—an era in whose development and publication he is something of an expert. An Atlantic crossing can be very tedious, if the winds are unhelpful, and we spent a good deal of time together in earnest discussion. When the ship docked at Southampton, he invited me to stay for a while at Burnt Oak Lodge, and I accepted. Although I came to Paris soon afterwards, I have been back to visit him twice more. He is somewhat stranded now, because his parents died, one after the other, not long after my first visit, consigning the care of Imogen and Esmeralda to him."

"Esmeralda?" she queried. "Was she named after Hugo's heroine, perhaps?"

"Impossible," I assured her, "given that she was born before *Notre-Dame de Paris* was published. I trust that she will be every bit as charming as Hugo's heroine when she is grown, though—and might even have the opportunity to dance with a black goat, given that the land on the seaward side the lodge, where the bulk of the estate lies, is not fit for growing crops, or grazing any better livestock than a small herd of goats and a flock of exotic sheep. Apart from those animals and three aged servants, I fear that the girls have little human company, for the hamlet that once accompanied the Lodge was deserted half a century ago, and they are still too young to enter into society in Pitsea. They have a full mile to walk on Sundays to attend the parish church, the entire congregation of which can be counted on one's fingers and toes."

"It must be lonely for your friend, too."

"He goes up to London regularly, to visit the British Museum and the booksellers in the surrounding streets. He has a fine library of his own, which contains some interesting esoterica. My friend Auguste Dupin came with me on the occasion of my last visit, in order to examine the library, and pronounced himself envious of some of the rarer items—a concession he rarely feels obliged to make."

"But Monsieur Carstairs does not have a copy of *The Mad Trist*?"

"No, I don't believe that he has. He is less interested in the era's sparse fiction than its supposedly factual productions, although all printed books of the period are fascinating to him, and he would doubtless have secured a copy of *The Mad Trist* had he ever had the opportunity. My friend Edgar Poe must have found a copy after I left America, though, for he quoted it in one of his own stories."

"Did he read the last chapter?"

"I assume so, although the story is unclear on that point and I have never asked him about the book in any of my letters. At any rate, he has suffered no ill-effects. I am convinced that he is now on the threshold of literary greatness, merely waiting for the public to catch up with him—his work is ahead of its time, in its variety and its effects. You would love it, I think. Hopefully, he will soon find a translator equal to the task of rendering his prose into French."

"And his love life is happy too?"

I thought that an odd remark, as well as an impertinent one, but I realized that she was still intrigued by the notion of a "mad trist" and the possibility that readers of the book might somehow be endangered.

"Yes," I said. "He is married to his cousin Virginia. Her health is not good, but they love one another very dearly—I might even say madly, were I not afraid of giving the wrong impression. She is young, and her constitution will hopefully become more robust as she matures. If so, they will have a long, prosperous and happy life together, as they richly deserve."[1]

"I'm glad to hear it," she said. "It seems, then, that you have nothing to fear from reading the book—and I feel well enough in myself to be willing to take the risk. Perhaps you might read a little of the story to me, given that the volume itself is far too valuable for you to lend out?"

"I would be glad to do so," I told her, "although I fear that the crossing will not last long enough for us to come near to the final chapter. I presume that you will be taking the London mail-coach when we dock, whereas I shall be taking a coach to Gravesend, and then a ferry across the Thames to Tilbury."

"It will not matter," she told me. "Once I have heard the opening of the story, I shall be able to improvise an appropriate ending of my own; all romances, after all, have much the same trajectory. The hero sets off on his quest, outwits and slays various adversaries, and in the end achieves betrothal—probably moved as much by divine madness as by chivalrous duty, although the texts are often too modest to say so."

Some of Dupin's pedantry had rubbed off on me. "Authentic Medieval romances are not like that," I said. "They often end tragically, like the story of Tristan and Iseult or the *Chanson de Roland*. Imitation romances are, however, far more prone to happy endings, for they are consciously written to please an audience, and audiences love happy endings. I doubt that *The Mad Trist* would have that title if its protagonist, Ethelred, did not eventually arrive at his fated rendezvous...but the adjective

---

1. This hope proved far too optimistic, alas; Virginia Poe died on 30th January 1847. I do not believe that Poe ever recovered from the blow, and effectively died of a broken heart, less than three years later. Nor do I believe, of course, that reading *The Mad Trist* could possibly have had anything to do with those tragic circumstances.

"mad" hints at the possibility that the rendezvous in question is no simple lovers' meeting, and might have an unfortunate outcome."

"We are wasting valuable time," she said, chiding me for my loquaciousness. "Read to me, please."

And so I read to her, opening the pages of *The Mad Trist* and beginning the first chapter. It was not easy, given the archaic style in which the book was printed, but the text itself was not nearly as awkward as the euphuistic prose extravaganzas typical of the period, and I did a first-rate job of deciphering it swiftly enough to maintain a modest but adequate pace in my oration.

It soon became apparent that the passages quoted by Poe must be further on in the text; it was obvious that he and Roderick Usher had not started at the beginning on the fateful occasion of their last *tête-à-tête*. It soon became apparent, too, that the story's trajectory would not be as simple as Madame Poyet had anticipated, for it was established very early on that Ethelred could not be entirely sure what awaited him at the end of his adventures. The early chapters introduced him not only to an innocent damsel in distress but to her sister, who was ambitious to be a witch. Ethelred, of course, sets forth to woo the virtuous sister, but soon becomes convinced that the witch, driven as much by envy as by lust, desires to prevent their union and claim him for herself. There was nothing particularly surprising in that, but what did astonish me, in a story first written down in the fifteenth century, was that there was a considerable ambiguity regarding the honesty of Ethelred's feelings, and it was hinted that, in allowing himself to be beguiled by the witch, he might be following his own true inclinations, perhaps unwittingly.

"That is most unusual," I commented to Madame Poyet, when I realized this and pointed it out to her. "Authentic romances are often tragic, but they rarely compromise with regard to the virtue of their heroes, or manifest any psychological depth of the kind that Victor Hugo imparts to his characters. Arthurian legendry—which, as I'm sure you know, is Norman in origin rather than Anglo-Saxon—goes to extraordinary lengths in holding its heroes accountable to rigid moral standards, finding only one of the knights of the round table worthy to touch the grail, although the others are undoubtedly good men."

"But the author of the book is named after Lancelot," Madame Poyet pointed out, "who falls in love with the king's beloved wife, thus soiling his virtue—and hers—irredeemably. He, at least, is a complex character, in terms of the inner turmoil of his guilt."

"True," I admitted. "And the hero of *The Mad Trist* is called Ethelred, which is as un-Norman a name as one can imagine. Nor is he a knight—although his author claims to be—or a nobleman, hence owing no formal allegiance of the baronial code of chivalry. Given all that, one is entitled to wonder whether the reckoning for which he is heading—whether or not it will involve a betrothal—might not be with the witch rather than his professed lady-love."

That possibility, however, appeared to be set aside when I read on, for the witch is summarily slain by Ethelred before he sets out on his adventurous journey: a narrative twist that startled both my auditor and myself.

"But death is not necessarily final in fiction," Madame Poyet reminded me. "In fiction, the dead can return at the meager cost of the author writing that they have risen from the tomb."

In "The Fall of the House of Usher", as I remembered only too well, Roderick's dead sister Madeleine returns from the tomb, having been subjected to a premature burial, and the passages quoted from *The Mad Trist* serve as an odd kind of "musical accompaniment" to her return, the sounds described in the texts echoing those she makes in emerging from her coffin and her crypt. I explained this to Madame Poyet, but my description of the text must have been awkward, or overly ambiguous.

"But your friend the author cannot have meant to imply that the resonance was mere coincidence," she said. "Surely, it must be the reading of the text that summons the dead woman from the tomb, operating as a magic spell; it is the sounds she makes that are the echo of those is the quoted passages, not *vice versa*."

I did not see how she could contradict me, given that I had read the story and she had not, but she obviously had unlimited confidence in what she had previously described as her "instinct for these things".

"But Roderick Usher, whose senses have become overly acute by virtue of a hereditary neurasthenia, has already heard her scratching in her coffin for several days," I said. "The pattern of actual sounds precedes that formed by the ones described in the quotations."

"Now, that makes no sense at all," Madame Poyet declared, forthrightly. "If the brother had heard the sister struggling in her coffin, surely he would have run down to release her immediately, rather than delaying for days, and then sitting down with his friend to read a silly romance."

It was a good point. I could not bring myself to explain to a lady that the implication carefully buried within my friend's text is that Roderick is burdened by guilt, presumably occasioned by an incestuous relationship with his sister, and that the last thing in the world he wants is to release her from her tomb so that she might confront him with the consequences of his sin. Unfortunately, I could not think of any other way to counter her criticism.

"But perhaps the sister's apparent resurrection is all delusion," Madame Poyet added. "Perhaps nothing really happens at all, except for a horrific vision inspired by reading *The Mad Trist*. Stories can do that, you know—there's nothing like a well-crafted story for inspiring dreams or nightmares. That's why so many readers prefer happy endings—they're defending themselves against the possibility of having bad dreams."

I could easily believe that Madeleine's resurrection was illusory—obviously, no such thing had actually happened when Poe had visited his friend—and I knew perfectly well that Poe's intention in adding such embellishments was to inspire dreams and nightmares, but I was not so sure that happy endings were a sound defence against bad dreams. That had not been my experience, as a reader or a dreamer. Alas, there was no time for me to develop a discussion along those lines, or to press on any further with the reading of *The Mad Trist*. The packet-boat was already gliding into Folkestone harbour, and it was time to prepare for disembarkation.

On the quay, I bid my new acquaintance farewell, and she thanked me very kindly for making the journey so pleasurable.

"I hope we shall meet again, as soon as possible, in London or in Paris," she said, "so that you can tell me what really happens in the final chapter of *The Mad Trist*. Until then, I suppose, I shall just have to trust in my imagination and my instinct."

She did not spell out what her imagination and instinct had told her about the terminus of Ethelred's adventure, but it had been sound enough in the diligence, when she had anticipated Esmeralda's doom in *Notre-Dame de Paris*, so I did not automatically assume that she would have been misled.

CHAPTER FOUR

The Essex Marshes by Night

My journey from Folkestone to Gravesend was uneventful, and the river crossing as comfortable as it was brief. The road eastwards from Tilbury was, however, in much worse condition than the roads on which the Boulogne diligence had been able to travel, and the pace of the journey was not helped at all by the gradual fall of darkness—which is by no means early in the month of May, but eventually inevitable. By the time I transferred from the local equivalent of a *patache* to Richard Carstairs' own fly, which he had dispatched to Pitsea to collect me, I felt that was black and blue from top to toe, and dog-tired.

I was not in a conversational mood, but I asked the servant who had brought the fly—he was the groundsman who tended to the family's livestock—whether Richard and his sisters were well, and was pleased to be told that they were all in the best of health. I remarked that the girls, at least, would be in bed asleep by the time I arrived, but I was assured that Imogen and Esmeralda had been exceedingly insistent that they be allowed to wait up to see me, and that Richard had been forced to bow to their will. I was flattered by their eagerness, for it implied that they still had pleasant memories of my last visit, and of myself.

While the groundsman steered the vehicle as cleverly as he could along the densely-hedged lanes, I cast my mind back to the last time I had seen Imogen and Esmeralda, and the smiles on their pretty faces. Those faces would have matured in the intervening three years, I knew, and were bound to have become even more beautiful, albeit a little more knowing. It was, however, Richard that I was going to see, and I forced myself to remember him too: his seriousness, his natural nobility of spirit, and his determination to give his little sisters the best education he could. I had no doubt that he would have done everything possible to further the final mission, even if it took valuable time away from his own pet project: the compilation of a history of the locale in which he lived, from late Medieval times to the era of the Romantic Movement, paying particular attention to the Elizabethan period.

The fly eventually pulled up before the house, which was situated on a low ridge running from west to east. The placid fresh water of the little lake, on the northern side of the rise, sparkled in the starlight; from that side of the house I could not see the salt marsh on the far side of the ridge, and the whole setting seemed idyllic, but I knew from past experience that the house was on a borderland, and that the southerly landscape was a good deal more barbaric. The house itself seemed a little gloomy as I dismounted in its shadow, by virtue of having only one lighted window in the ground floor—that of Richard's study, where he and the girls were presumably sitting up waiting for me, gathered around a dying fire. The weather was not very cold, to tell the truth, but there was an east wind blowing, which carried a chill, and the twin plumes of smoke escaping from the chimney stack told me that there was more than one fire lit within—the other, presumably, being in the kitchen range.

My welcome was as extravagant as I could have hoped. Richard was exactly as I had seen him last, sturdy and upright, but, as I had anticipated, his two sisters had altered considerably in growing older. Imogen, who was now almost twenty, had become every inch a lady, possessed of poise as well as beauty, and a perfect politeness in her manner that could not quite conceal the enthusiasm of her greeting as she met my eyes, smiling. She blushed rose-pink when I kissed her cheek. Esmeralda, who had not long turned sixteen, did not bother with any such pretence of etiquette, but flung her arms around me and gave vent to her glee in giggling laughter. Both girls were dark-haired, as befit remote descendants of the island's Norman conquerors, but Imogen was a rich brunette whose glossy tresses had a hint of chestnut about them, while Esmeralda's languid curls were almost black. Paradoxically, Imogen's eyes were a darker brown than her sister's; the latter's irises were much brighter, with a remarkable golden sheen, like that imparted to precious metal by dutiful polishing.

Once the initial greetings were complete, Richard was quick to hasten his wards to their beds; they only mounted a token rebellion before consenting, meekly enough, in exchange for the promise that they would see much more of me on the morrow. They bore away stout wax candles set in broad trays, which doubtless gave the house a more cheerful aspect, as seen from outside—at least for a little while.

"I've put you in your usual room, facing southwards," Carstairs said. "Your trunk will be unpacked by the time you go up. Do you need something to eat?"

"I had a dinner of sorts in Tilbury," I told him, "but I'd gladly drink a glass of brandy. Considering that Essex is so flat, its roads are punishing."

"The marshes are flat enough," he agreed, as he filled my glass and handed it to me, "but there's no shortage of high ground in the vicinity, and the permanent roads run over the surer ground. In the gathering gloom, you might not have been able to take full account of the fact that the road from Pitsea goes up and then down again, with several undulations in between—to be honest, though, the dryness of the road more than makes up for its unevenness. Driving across the pathways of the marsh in a fly is a hazardous business, for the wheels are always likely to become enmired; it's well-nigh impossible in a heavier vehicle. That's why I always walk when I'm abroad on that side of the ridge, whenever I go out hunting for duck, or fishing in the estuary, or merely to survey my paltry domain."

There was no point in asking him about hunting, given that it was the close season, and I abhor fishing tales; I was, in any case, far more enthusiastic to know how his scholarship was progressing."

"Slowly," he told me. "I've made voluminous notes, but I haven't actually started writing the book yet. I've consulted the parish and court records for miles around, although they're rather patchy in many places. Cromwell's vandals did more than break idols when they invaded the local churches, alas, so there's a dark curtain hanging over the early seventeenth century and all of the sixteenth."

"No news, then of the mysterious witch of the Burnt Oak?"

"Nothing written—but I've revised my opinion slightly as to the plausibility of the story. If one works purely from the official records, one might easily get the impression that Essex was hardly touched by the witch-craze—there's no hard evidence that even the notorious Matthew Hopkins was ever involved in more than one trial, and an over-scrupulous researcher would doubtless conclude that his reputation as an itinerant witchfinder was purely a result of malicious slander. If one looks beyond official documentation, however—especially if one consults manuscript diaries, as I have done in aristocratic houses a good deal grander than this one—a different picture emerges. There was a considerable fear of witches in the late sixteenth century, which flared up more than once—but any actions to which it gave rise had to be private and clandestine rather than public and legal, for there were no Dominican inquisitors hereabouts once Bloody Mary was dead and Elizabeth came to the throne. Witch-hunting was officially frowned upon in England, especially after Scot had published his skeptical demolition of the whole idea."

I was exhausted, and the brandy was helping to soothe my aches somewhat, but I could not help querying: "Scot?"

"Reginald Scot. He published his *Discoverie of Witchcraft* in 1584, mocking all belief in magic, and belief in witchcraft in particular, in no uncertain terms. Champions of the so-called New Learning took the lesson to heart, convinced by the book's arguments, and began to pretend that they'd always thought along the same lines—but there was a backlash too, from believers who thought that they were being insulted as well as contradicted, and charges of heresy were brought. Such accusations could still be direly dangerous at the time, but Scot had helped his brother Michael and Thomas Digges, who were the finest engineers in the land, to rebuild the defences of Dover, and he was under Navy protection. Ironically, the most visible remaining evidence of Scot's endeavors is found in the fanciful literature of the day, where the spells that he quoted in order to mock their absurdity were adopted into Shakespeare's *Macbeth* and other melodramas produced by the various London companies. At any rate, the possibility of any formal prosecution for witchcraft succeeding between 1584 and the end of the century, at least within earshot of London, was virtually negligible. Things were very different in Scotland, where a widespread and long-lasting panic was provoked by the trial of the North Berwick witches in 1590, prompting James VI to write his *Daemonologie*, but in London, official witch-hunting was out of the question, and remained so even after James VI became James I of England as well—although he did order, far too late, that all surviving copies of the *Discoverie* should be burned. In England, local panics had to be handled informally, and carefully hushed up—save for their folkloristic echoes."

"So you now think that, even though no record remains but for *folkloristic echoes*, a witch might really have been burned on the site where the house now stands?"

"Not burned—that would have been far too risky—but hanged, quite possibly...after being ducked in the pool, probably. The tree might have been burned thereafter, though, for fear that it might have been cursed by the witch's dying imprecations."

"And the burning would have put an end to any such curse, in popular belief?"

"Perhaps—it was probably done more in hope than expectation, given that rumors of her ghost persisted across the generations. The estuary mists are conducive to ghost sightings, of course, especially with my sheep and goats roaming free in the marsh. I've done some actual digging, of course, as any good antiquarian would. The house has good foundations and a well-made cellar, but it's not too difficult to find the remains of roots that were let alone when the trunk of an ancient oak was levelled…including fragments that don't seem quite dead, although it's difficult to imagine that living cells could lie dormant underground for more than two hundred years.

I could not help remembering Madame Poyet's instinct, and what it had told her about a witch being ducked and hanged, and then the tree from which she had been suspended being burned. I laughed, though, and tapped the pocket of my overcoat. "We must save the stories of the supernatural for tomorrow, when the girls can provide an appreciative audience. I have a treat for you: I have in my possession a copy of *The Mad Trist* by Sir Launcelot Canning."

He had obviously heard of the book, presumably from other sources as well as reading "The Fall of the House of Usher"—a copy of which I had sent him, although it had also been printed in *Bentley's Miscellany*. His immediate response was that of any true bibliophile. "Is it for me?" he asked, avidly.

I regretted having to disappoint him, but it was necessary. "I fear not," I said. "It was given to me to hand on our mutual friend Auguste Dupin—but I was already on my way to the *Messageries*, and had to bring it with me, promising to deliver it when I return."

"Oh!" he said, unable to conceal his chagrin. "Dupin!" The way he pronounced the name made it seem that he disapproved of the Chevalier, but I presumed that the bile in his tone was merely the envy of one bibliophile who had just been bested by another.

"In the meantime, though," I said, "we shall have free use of it. I shall read it to you and the girls, if you wish—although it might take several nights to complete the lecture."

Carstairs did not seem to care overmuch whether I read the story aloud or not. The object interested him more than the tale it contained. His once-strong interest in Romantic literature had waned to a greater extent than my own as he had become increasingly isolated from society and more obsessive in his historical research. Even Shakespeare's goriest tragedy, it seemed, was now interesting to him primarily because of its borrowings from some skeptical engineer.

"The girls will love it," I added, to shore up my case.

"Of course they will," he agreed, in a desultory manner. "I'm looking forward to it myself—but you must be very tired. You'll feel much better after a good night's sleep. We can go out in the morning for a healthy walk. The surroundings haven't changed a bit—and probably haven't changed much in centuries."

"Except for the burning of the legendary oak, the building of your house and the dereliction of the other dwellings in the vicinity," I reminded him.

"Except for that," he agreed, and showed me upstairs to my room—although I remembered the way quite well.

I wasted no time in getting ready for bed and lying down, although I left a candle burning on the night-stand to serve as a nightlight.

I did not fall asleep as quickly as I might have hoped, but drifted off eventually, still beset by nagging aches and twinges. Unsurprisingly, I dreamed—not of witches or ghosts, but once again of Madame Poyet.

Again, I am forced to gloss over the central substance of my dream, and it is with some embarrassment that I mention some of its supplementary features. Most importantly, I heard what appeared to be a voice whispering in my ear—although, when I turned my head to see who was speaking there was no one there—which told me repeatedly that there was nothing wrong in what my dream-self was doing, thinking or feeling.

"The lady is a Parisienne, after all," the voice said, "and her husband is in commerce, which obliges him to travel a good deal. It is unlikely in the extreme that he remains celibate when they are apart, or that she does. If she married him for money as is highly likely, then she probably keeps some young dandy as a *cicisbeo*, to decorate her arm when she goes to the opera and warm her bed. You have read Balzac's novels, and you know how the Parisian *monde* operates. Everything is permitted, provided that appearances are maintained. Even if she has some such popinjay at her beck and call, though, she must hunger for intelligent conversation and intellectual stimulation, like the Marquise du Châtelet, who loved Voltaire passionately in spite of his ugliness. Madame Poyet is an admirer of the novels of George Sand, and she loved Alfred de Vigny's account of an angel who sets out to redeem Satan and is seduced by him instead. What more insight into her true character could you possibly want? Even if she has only read about such things, her reading has evidently made her a convert, worming its way into her soul and arming its passions. She has told you the name of the hotel at which she will be staying in London, which is only a few hours away by coach, and expressed the hope of seeing you again very soon—what is that if not an open invitation to debauchery?"

I must hasten to add that this kind of hallucination is not at all typical of my dreams, let alone my ideas. I am not at all given to hearing voices, let alone the kind of insidious voices that remind one of the old legend about the Devil appointing an imp to sit incessantly on a man's left shoulder, to engage in a perpetual battle of wits with a guardian angel stationed to his right. In any case, the voice that was speaking in my dream came neither from the left nor the right, but from directly behind me—as if I had some strange shadow-self perpetually dogging my footsteps.

In order to banish the voice and put Madame Poyet out of my mind, I made a deliberate effort, in the intervals between my dozing, to think of other things. In particular, I tried to think about my host—not about his historical researches, which had some slightly sinister associations, but about the quietness of his life here in this relatively lonely spot, free from all the stresses that afflict quotidian life in a great city like Paris. I thought about his walking, his bird-hunting and fishing, his desultory farming activities, and his peaceful domestic life, in the glorious and energetic company of his two lovely sisters....

That was a mistake, alas, for I had no sooner began to think about the loveliness of Richard's two sisters than the images of my dream were drawn once again in an indecent direction. This time, I fought with all the might of my chivalrous conscience, but the insidious voice immediately returned to the fray, inevitably weighing in on the side of temptation.

"Do you really think that they are any more innocent than Madame Poyet?" the voice demanded. "In deed, they must be virginal still, but in thought, how can they be? They are children no more, and the lusts of the flesh have blossomed within them, all the more avidly for having no ready outlet? Why do you think they have been looking forward to your arrival? Why do you think that they were so very glad to see you? Did you not see that they are already entering into a competition for your attention? Do you not understand that their competition is bound to intensify, until they are ready to tear one another to pieces for the honor of being debauched by you? And why should you choose, except to decide which one to favor first? You have time enough to delight them both. It is not merely your privilege but your duty, for the consequences of leaving them tantalized might be even direr. There is no fault involved, for they are conscious and determined enchantresses, intent on your seduction."

In the end, I could bear it no longer, and I dreamed that I stood up to my full height and howled: "Get thee behind me, Saint-Germain!"—but I did not know whether I was addressing the impostor or the metaphorical suburb, and, in any case, the voice was already behind me, so there was no defense in the injunction.

I had only one recourse left to me, then, and that was to think about Auguste Dupin, the most knowledgeable and most virtuous man in Paris—but that only prompted me to think about the murders in the Rue Morgue, and the hideous state of the corpse stuffed up the chimney, and the monstrous ape that had committed the crime.

"But it was not a crime at all," the voice told me, "for the ape was only following his nature, acting in accordance with his instinct—and is he not our cousin, according to the theory of the Chevalier de Lamarck? Are we not apes ourselves, who have lost most of our hair, but only part of our instinct? Do we not have our own impulses to violence? Why are the seven deadly sins so dangerous to our morals if they are not engraved in our flesh, requiring the utmost efforts of our powers of reason and virtue to withstand them? And who, in the final analysis, really contrives to suppress them? Do you think that even Auguste Dupin can make his way direct to Heaven, given the things that he has done and the tenor of his thinking? If the lustful and the avaricious really go to Hell, then all of Paris must have been rebuilt in the Inferno by now, its suburbs sprawling well beyond the limits of the Dantean circles. If the slothful and the gluttonous are there too, how could there ever be imps enough at Satan's command to torment them all? And if even Purgatory were reserved for men of great intellect and men of colossal virtue, must it not be exceedingly crowded even so? We are but creatures of appetite, deep down—and who can blame us for seeking satiation, when the world is so full of provocation and invitation? Voluptuousness is all around us, in the wilds of Essex as in the heart of Paris; what chance does virtue have when such appeal is made to our baser nature, to the orang-utan that is the collective soul of humankind? The Rue Morgue is, after all, where we all end up, chilled and exposed to protect us from the risk of premature burial. But is not every burial premature? Does not every man die while hardly having lived? What fools we are, while living for such a brief hour, to refuse what life has to offer us! Reach out, reach out, and pluck the fruit... especially the forbidden fruit, which is the sweetest of all. Live! Love!"

I raged against that voice, and would have murdered the speaker had I only been able to lay my hands upon any but a ghost or shadow. I cursed the gentile night that had brought me such horrors—but I did not fully wake up until the sunlight was streaming through my window, long after what ought to have been the merciful first light of dawn.

CHAPTER FIVE
The Essex Marshes by Day

Confronted by a breakfast of smoked herring and eggs, served with toast and butter—and an abundant supply of tea— by Richard's patient housemaid, I felt a great deal better, and put the night's torments squarely behind me. My aches and pains had eased considerably.

While the meal was slowly consumed the two girls plagued me with all manner of questions about Paris, about its society and its fashions. Most of them I could not answer, but they did not seem very disappointed, merely changing the grounds of their interrogation in the hope of finding common ground on which we could all become excited.

Imogen, who was apparently able to read French and made full use of that license, asked me whether I had ever met George Sand or Alexandre Dumas. I had to admit that I had not yet met either of them, prompting Esmeralda—to whom her sister presumably read aloud on occasion—to ask me whether I did not attend *cénacles* on a regular basis, seemingly assuming that everyone in Paris did so. That forced me to explain that I was not really a seasoned inhabitant of the rather specialized micro-cosm of literary salons and *cénacles*, although I sometimes saw famous writers at a distance while shopping for books. I hesitated to mention that I had met Honoré de Balzac, lest I be obliged to explain the circumstances in which I had done so.

My observations on the restoration of Notre-Dame did not interest my inquisitors, alas, but when Imogen mentioned the

Philosophical Harmonic Society of Paris, and I admitted that I had been talking to its President only the day before last, they did become enthused—until Richard cut the discussion short, opining that Rosicrucianism was not a fit subject for feminine consideration. I dared not ask him whether he or his sisters had read *Zanoni*.

Imogen and Esmeralda were enthusiastic to accompany us on our walk, but Richard forbade them, saying that he intended to take me through the marsh to the seashore, and that it might be treacherous underfoot. They were quick to remind him of the promise he had made the night before, and he was equally quick to counter that they could have me to themselves in the after-noon, and that we would all go for a walk together the following morning, on the safer side of the ridge. He added that he and I needed to catch up on serious matters of mutual interest before giving ourselves over to a deluge of silliness. Even I thought the last remark a trifle unfair, not to say insulting, but his sisters were good girls deep down, and wanted to make a good impression on me, so they accepted the decision—after extracting a further promise that we would all four spend the evening together, and that they could entertain us with their musical recitals.

Richard and I strode off in our Wellington boots through the grounds of the house, whose lack of an enclosing wall on the seaward side made it difficult to determine where the grounds ended and the miry marsh began. We took his two border collies with us—with the result that the few scrawny sheep and goats that caught sight of us scampered anxiously away, in fear of harassment.

The tide was out, but we reached the edge of the mud-flats soon enough, where we veered to the left in order to follow the coast in the direction of the ruins of Hadleigh Castle and the fishing-port of Leigh. There were sanderlings and oyster-catchers busy probing the mud for shellfish, but the predomi-nant sound was the mournful piping of curlews.

"Are we still on your land?" I asked him, when we had drawn away from the house by a furlong or so."

"If you can call it land," he said. "When a storm surge is added to a spring tide, the sea comes lapping at the foot of the ridge, almost as far as my back doorstep, evidently believing all of this to be part of Neptune's domain—but insofar as this unpromising mud is subject to ownership, it's mine for nearly a mile. The grasses that grow here are salt-tolerant species, though, and don't make good grazing, except for certain eccentric breeds of sheep. The bushes are no better, and although my little flock of goats seems to have become accustomed to them over the generations, they much prefer grazing the succulent leaves on the shore of the lake, when they're allowed to stray." He pointed to the frolicking dogs and added: "You might not think it to look at them now, but they're hard workers, and past masters in gathering and herding the flocks. Are you, by any chance, carrying that book you mentioned to me in your pocket?"

"Why, yes," I said, slightly surprised by the abrupt change of subject. I moved rather hastily to extract the volume, and it caught on the flap of my pocket. As I yanked it free, something white was flipped out of the pocket and fluttered down to the ground. It was a crumpled and slightly grubby visiting card. Richard paused and picked it up; he was in the process of handing it back to me when his eyes fell upon the lettering inscribed there.

"How on Earth do you know Coningsby?" he asked.

"He accosted me at the *Messageries* as I was about to board the diligence," I said. "He wanted to buy the book." I held up *The Mad Trist* so that there could be no ambiguity about which book I meant, and then added: "How do *you* know him?"

"I don't, really," he said, laughing. "Although, if he ever saw me holding a book he wanted, I dare say that I'd make his acquaintance rapidly enough. Those are the only circumstances in which he's inclined to talk to people—in a manner utterly devoid of etiquette, so I hear. He's not a bad man—probably as virtuous as you or I—but he has no skill at all in the social graces, and when his attention is fixed on a book, all considerations of politeness and decency seem to become irrelevant to him. He's a regular in the reading room at the Museum,[2] where our eyes could hardly help but meet and our elbows have jostled on occasion, but the rule of silence has always prohibited us from speaking to one another. I dare say that he knows my name, just as I know his, but he's by far the more notorious of the two of us—a virtual legend in our little community of scholars. He's a crackpot, of course...but it's understandable that he prefers to label himself a bibliomaniac."

"What kind of crackpot?" I demanded, remembering my anxiety that Coningsby might easily be able to discover my identity, and follow me to England.

"Oh, the kind that believes in the great conspiracy that saved England from the Armada, and the *Black Book* that was supposedly printed in its wake. He's been searching for it all his adult life—it's his version of the Holy Grail. There are many other titles on his list of desiderata, of course...but I had not known that *The Mad Trist* was one of them. May I?"

I handed over the volume reflexively, and he promptly flipped it open to the title page. "Ah!" he said. "Printed by the Widow Orwin, evidently for Joan Broome. That might explain his interest."

"How so?" I asked, completely mystified.

"Because the two ladies in question are commonly cited in the hypothetical list of the conventicle's membership. That was inevitable: they were both widows who had inherited their husbands' businesses, and positions of considerable influence therewith. Joan Orwin had been married three times, I believe, to three different printers, all of whom were deceased; how could a woman in that situation not be suspected of witchcraft? Nothing could be done about it, of course, given the intellec-

---

2. To avoid any possible confusion on the part of my readers, I ought to note that Carstairs was referring to the old reading room at the British Museum, which was a good deal more cramped and uncomfortable than the new one commissioned shortly thereafter by the Keeper of the Printed Books, construction of which began in 1854.

tual climate of the day. Broome was the more powerful of the two Joans—by 1595 or thereabouts, her establishment at the sign of the Green Dragon was the leading bookseller in London, able to influence the reception of virtually any printed book... and to determine whether a book was printed at all. That was bound to generate all manner of spiteful rumor, but Broome was untouchable, having all the aspirant authors in the Court effectively at her mercy, perhaps including Elizabeth herself. Those speculators who believe that the great conspiracy was led by a woman invariably point to her, if they stop short of the ultimate boldness of accusing the queen."

"I don't understand," I protested. "What great conspiracy? I never heard of a great conspiracy in that era."

"Probably because it's a pure myth—an antiquarians' fantasy. As if there were not enough puzzles and mysteries in history without concocting more! The core of the myth is the great storm that destroyed the Spanish Armada, and saved England from ruinous invasion. The English Church, Court and Parliament were quick to claim that the storm was an Act of God, performed to save a proud protestant nation from Catholic ire, but counterclaims were made even at the time, if only in whispers—claims that the storm had actually been whipped up by a conventicle of witches. Storm-raising was a particularly controversial issue at the time—Reginald Scot had ridiculed the notion, but the North Berwick witches were charged with whipping up a storm intended to kill King James and his new bride as they returned from Copenhagen, and James was apparently convinced that they really had done so.

"You can understand easily enough how the Catholics who had been briefly favored under Mary, only to be persecuted again, with renewed fervor, when Elizabeth came to the throne, had an interest in suggesting that the storm was the Devil's work rather than God's—and they, of course, took it for granted that witches were the Devil's minions, commissioned to do his work on Earth while his demons were imprisoned in Hell. This was the Tudor era, however, when disputes emerging from the

Reformation were further complicated by the claims of the New Learning—the march of science, in our modern terminology—and a further counterclaim appears to have been put about, also clandestinely, that although a conventicle of witches *was* responsible for the destruction of the Armada, they were not Satan's minions at all, but exponents of a new kind of alchemy, who were in the process of discovering and beginning to unleash the latent powers of the human mind…and, as a corollary, the latent powers of print."

"Print?" I queried. "What *latent powers of print?*"

"You have to remember the context in which this was happening. Although printing was not a new technology—more than a hundred years had passed since Caxton had set up his pioneering press in London—it was just hovering on the threshold of democratization, as aristocrats and merchants began routinely to have their sons taught to read, and often their wives and daughters too. Printed books were no longer esoteric, and were thus coming to be regarded as dangerous. This was not long after the first influx of printed bibles into England, during Mary's reign, which had prompted the burning of books, their sellers, and their printers alike, on a considerable scale.

"That control had been relaxed under Elizabeth—but the relaxation that let in the Bible also let in all manner of other texts. Pamphleteering became a popular political sport, and books soon came to be regarded with extreme trepidation, as possible agents of social and spiritual revolution. In 1586, the Archbishop of Canterbury, John Whitgift, persuaded the Star Chamber to issue an edict forbidding all publication without approval by the Ecclesiastical authorities. His primary targets were Catholic and Puritan pamphlets, which were attacking the Church of England from two opposed flanks, but the edict's effect was much more widespread, driving a considerable sector of publishing underground and tarring all of the proscribed texts with the same Satanic brush—even proto-novels like *The Mad Trist*, whose prosecution and condemnation was evidently belated.

"Ecclesiastical censorship affected a great many of the leading intellectuals of the day, who were virtually forced to enter into conspiracies of a sort, simply to circulate their less orthodox ideas. Secret colleges were formed, where honest intellectuals discussed the natural and occult sciences alike in anxious whispers. Those modern antiquarians who take it for granted that any grand conspiracy of the witches of London would have required a male leader usually point the finger at John Dee, although others identify Reginald Scot, or his brother, and some the Earl of Oxford."

"John Dee the wizard?" I queried, vaguely.

"His modern reputation as a wizard in based on a sensational and scurrilous book published long after his death, advertising his brief relationship with a skryer named Edward Kelley. Dee was certainly interested in the so-called occult sciences as well as all other branches of the New Learning, but his primary reputation at the time of the Armada was as England's greatest mathematician. Like Scot, he was under the protection of the Navy, because he trained their officers in the art and science of navigation, as he did the seamen of various companies associated with the Merchant Adventurers' Guild, including those searching for the North-East and North-West Passages. That work left little impact on history because it was protected by strict secrecy, lest the Spanish and the Dutch acquire a similar mastery of navigation. We don't know whether the English captains of the time were yet equipped with telescopes, thanks to Dee's ward and collaborator Tom Digges—the man who worked with the Scots on Dover's defences—because that would have been the most precious state secret of all."

All of this was rather confusing and somewhat overwhelming, although the casual surfeit of information was entirely typical of a historian's enthusiasm—especially a historian who spent so much time isolated in the Essex marshes, with only his sisters, servants and meager flocks for company.

"But what is this *Black Book* for which Coningsby is searching?" I demanded, trying to get back to the original issue.

"Nobody seems very sure. As the overwhelming likelihood is that no such book exists, you're probably at liberty to make up your own tale. The general idea, however, is that the company of storm-raisers—and we ought not to neglect the possibility, however slim, that there really was a secret company of individuals who sincerely believed that they had raised the storm—were flushed with their success, and tried to take advantage of the status they had acquired to produce a book that would concentrate and focus the supposed magical power of print...a kind of alchemy of the printed word. Most of those who tell the story represent the volume in question as a grimoire—a book of magic spells—or as an alchemical text-book, but again, opinions vary, and you're probably free to make up your own account. What Coningsby believes the *Black Book* to be is anyone's guess...but his interest in this volume is certainly intriguing."

As he was speaking, Richard had done what I had done when I first inspected the volume, turning first to the beginning of the text, and then back to the flyleaf. He stopped dead in his tracks and said: "Aha!" To judge by his tone, he might equally well have cried: "Eureka!"

This time, mercifully, I knew exactly what it was to which he was reacting, and even knew why. "The inscription does make that particular copy doubly interesting," I commented. "Jane Anger was the pseudonym of the great Elizabethan feminist, I believe—although it is conceivable that the inscription was added by another Jane Anger."

Carstairs looked at me in frank amazement, as if he could hardly believe that I was party to such esoteric information. I felt proud, although I took slight offense at the fact that he had underestimated me by such a wide margin. "Have you read Jane Anger's pamphlet?" he asked.

"No," I admitted, reluctantly.

"Do you know who printed it?"

"The Widow Orwin?" I guessed.

"Her husband, Thomas Orwin," Carstairs countered, as if

scoring a point in a game of wits. "In 1589—the year after the Armada. He had earlier printed the misogynistic pamphlet to which it was a reply. In my estimation, he was merely trying to cash in on a controversy that he had stirred up deliberately, in order to promote his wares—but that still leaves the question of who actually wrote the Jane Anger pamphlet unanswered. Thomas Ortwin might well have written it himself, but if not...."

"Then Joan Orwin is the likeliest candidate," I chipped in, eager to regain the intellectual high ground. "Unless, of course, it was Queen Elizabeth herself!"

I had not meant the second suggestion seriously, but one should never underestimate the venturesome spirit of serious antiquarians. "Those are the most commonly advanced hypotheses," Richard confirmed, pensively.

Eager to get ahead of him in the game, I said: "If the Queen of England was Jane Anger the feminist, perhaps she was also Sir Launcelot Canning the romancer. Perhaps the assertion that the printed book is reproduced from a manuscript of 1450 or thereabouts is deliberate misdirection, to conceal the fact that it was actually composed in the early 1590s...if not by Elizabeth, then by the Widow Orwin or Joan Broome." Carstairs had, after all, explicitly invited me to make up my own tale in order to add an extra twist to the Gordian knot of historical and bibliographical mystery.

"That *is* an interesting possibility," he mused—but was quick to add: "The possibility that *The Mad Trist* was composed in 1593, I mean, not the possibility that Elizabeth was its author. On the other hand, the possibility that Jane Anger and Sir Launcelot Canning might be one and the same...."

"And if the Widow Orwin really was a witch," I said, getting completely carried away, "perhaps she was the same one who was hanged or burnt at the very spot where your house now stands."

"Don't be ridiculous," my companion said, rather sharply. "Records survive of the deaths of Joan Orwin and Joan Broome they both perished before Elizabeth's reign ended, without leaving London."

"It must have been some minor member of the great conspiracy, then," I said, "or perhaps its unidentified leader."

Carstairs sighed in mock-despair, and handed *The Mad Trist* back to me. I returned it to my pocket, and we both began walking again. After a pause for thought, he asked: "What did Coningsby say to you, exactly?"

I recounted the full story of the strange encounter at the *Messageries*, including the injunction that Coningsby had shouted after the departing diligence. I expected my friend to fall upon that bizarre circumstance, but instead, he asked: "How did Coningsby know that you had the book?"

"He saw Saint-Germain give it to me."

"Yes, you told me that much—but how did he know what book it was that Saint-Germain handed over, if he was watching from a distance?"

"I assume that Saint-Germain only had the one book on his person, and that Coningsby knew what it was because he had been tracking it for some time. Perhaps he saw it handed to Saint-Germain, just as he saw it handed to me. Saint-Germain implied that it had not been in his possession for long, and that he had thought of sending it to Dupin as soon as he found it."

"But this false mage is a collector himself?"

"Of books on magic and mesmerism, certainly—but he told me in so many words that he was not the kind of man to hoard a book in his library simply because it was rare."

"Is there any other kind of book-collector? There's something fishy about this, my friend. Coningsby might be right—Saint-Germain might have tricked you."

"I did wonder about that," I admitted. "But why? Why should he have wanted to send the book to England—and, if he did, why should he resort to chicanery to persuade me to bring it?"

"I haven't the slightest idea," Carstairs conceded.

"We *are* going to read it, though, aren't we?" I said. "All the way through, including the final chapter?"

"Of course," he said. "We know full well that there is no

power at all in curses. I wouldn't miss the opportunity for the world—if you'll consent to read it aloud, that is, while I listen."

"Most certainly," I said. "But what about your sisters? Should they be allowed to listen too?"

He frowned. "To be perfectly honest," he said, "I doubt that we'd be able to stop them. They've become quite uncontrollable of late, as you doubtless observed at breakfast. They made a show of obeying me then, but we're all well aware of the fact that they do as they please, and that I'm impotent to stop them. The days of patriarchy are doomed, my friend, within the family and without. I dare say that we poor menfolk will fight to the last ditch to preserve it, and it might take a century or more for its last relics to fade away, but the simple truth is that Jane Anger's descendants have won her cause. If I forbid Imogen and Esmeralda to listen to your reading, it will only make them all the more determined to hear every last word, by hook or by crook. If, on the other hand, I give them permission, there's at least a chance that they'll get bored long before the end, so that they'll absent themselves before we reach the supposedly-fateful final chapter—which might conceivably be unsuitable for their tender ears."

I was not convinced by the latter part of his argument, and my observation of his sisters' apparent meekness suggested that the first part was not entirely justified either. In any case, I rather liked the idea of Imogen and Esmeralda sitting quietly while I read to them, looking up at me admiringly as I entranced them with my eloquence...or, to be strictly accurate, with an oral eloquence supplementary to the humble efforts of Sir Launcelot Canning's dull print.

CHAPTER SIX
The Hearth of Burnt Oak Lodge

That afternoon, as had been promised, I spent with the two girls. The day was sunny, so we went outside—not, this time, toward the estuary, but to the other side of the house. The little lake was even lovelier than I remembered it, its placid waters green by virtue of the abundant water-weed lurking beneath the surface, in spite of their dutiful reflection of the blue sky. The verdure around its shores was similarly bright with the enthusiasm of spring. There were reeds growing around three-fourths of the shore, and there were numerous buntings nesting therein. The trees on the banks—mostly willows—were also replete with songbirds.

"I love the lake," Imogen told me. "Richard taught me to swim in its waters—but he will not let me swim in the estuary, for he says that the currents are far too dangerous. Here the water is still and shallow, quite benign, though somewhat cluttered with algae, especially at this time of year."

"I'm learning to swim too," Esmeralda immediately put in, not wanting to be outdone. "I'm determined to know how before summer arrives in all its torrid glory—although it tends to bring swarms of mosquitoes with it, which make stripping naked hazardous."

Imogen evidently disapproved of the casual mention of stripping naked, but Esmeralda only laughed at her sister's censorious frown.

"It must be wonderful, living in Paris," Imogen continued, in her scrupulously polite fashion, casually linking arms with me as we strolled along the shore. "The greatest city in the world, and the hub of civilization. How I would love to visit you there some day. Do you think that Richard would ever permit it?"

Again, Esmeralda was in haste to keep up. She grabbed my left arm rather more fervently than Imogen had taken possession of my right, and said: "Richard would never allow you to make such a journey alone, darling—nor with him, if it meant leaving me behind—but in a year or so, I shall be sufficiently grown-up for him to take us both. Then, my dear Monsieur, if we come, we may stay in your house, may we not? It is quite a large one, I understand."

"Large enough," I admitted, wryly amused by the mode of address.

"And on the edge of the Faubourg Saint-Germain," Imogen put in. Her reading of French fiction had obviously acquainted her with the *cachet* of that district. "We would be able to visit *salons.*"

"And *cénacles,*" Esmeralda countered.

I tried to explain that salons and *cénacles* were the kind of gatherings to which one had to be invited, or at least introduced by some *habitué*, but could not quite persuade them that I was not able to make such introductions myself. In any case, my attempted explanations only led to more extensive questioning about the protocols of Parisian society. Imogen raised the matter of the Harmonic Society again, but out of respect for Richard's desires I was very vague in my comments. I did, however, have some success in relating the stories of some of my less sensational adventures with Auguste Dupin, carefully omitting the murders in the Rue Morgue. Fortunately, they had not been allowed to read Poe, and did not press me on that point.

The impression I formed of the two girls, as we walked around the shore of the lake three times, anti-clockwise, was that they were perfectly charming, both striving with all their might to seem adult and ladylike—a contest in which Imogen inevitably had the upper hand, although Esmeralda kept a tight rein on her resentment and did not sulk at all.

When we returned to the house Richard asked me whether I would mind going down to the cellar with him, to help him bring up some provisions on behalf of the cook. I was glad to do so—but the hope that I might see any evidence of the ancient tree's roots, dead or alive, was dashed by the sheer crowding of the stores that were kept there, which included a coal-heap, a strange multitude of agricultural implements, and trunks full of old clothing, as well as sacks of grain and cases of wine.

In the evening, after an early dinner, we made our preparations for the promised evening of performances, which were to take place in the drawing-room. Imogen went first, playing the piano and singing a number of popular ballads and madrigals. Richard and I applauded with sincere enthusiasm, although it seemed to me that Esmeralda's applause was perfunctory. I put that down to nervousness on the younger sister's part, as it was now her turn to perform, to an audience that included a guest— and a guest from Paris, no less.

Esmeralda's instrument was the guitar—much less fashionable than the piano, and more challenging to the fingers. Understandably, she was less skilful than her sister, and her singing voice was not quite as perfect, but what struck me most about her performance was her choice of music. Although she sat quite still herself, she played several tunes that had obviously been composed to accompany dances—and not sedate waltzes, but Spanish dances of a markedly wild character. The songs she sang were all ballads, but not the familiar and traditional ballads that Imogen had selected; they were more passionate and poignant, occasionally plaintive. When the time came to applaud her, I was as enthusiastic as I had been before, but it seemed to me that Richard was noticeably less so, and Imogen—perhaps by way of retaliation—distinctly lacking in enthusiasm. Esmeralda did not seem to care about that; her eyes were fixed on me, as if mine were the only reaction that mattered.

"Where did you learn those extraordinary dance tunes and

barbarous songs?" I asked her.

"From one of Richard's books," she replied. "Not one of those he keeps locked in the cabinet, mind—although sometimes I suspect that he regrets his decision to leave it on the open shelves. There are not many English tunes written for the guitar, alas."

"It's your turn now," Imogen put in, fluttering the lashes of her dark eyes in my direction. "You promised to read to us. It has been a long time since you last read to us—or since anyone else read to us, for that matter. It doesn't count when it's just between ourselves."

"We can never agree on which books to read to one another," Esmeralda put in, "so we usually end up reading by ourselves. I love that—it's wonderful to be able to immerse oneself in a story—but I love hearing you read too."

Suitably flattered by their complimentary eagerness, I took *The Mad Trist* out of my pocket once again, and began reading. I began at the beginning, of course, so I was duplicating the text I had already read to Madame Poyet on the packet-boat, but I did not mind that. The repetition enabled me to be a little more relaxed, and to concentrate on my diction. I was able to put myself into the story a little more, and to prepare my tone for dramatic moments that I could now anticipate.

Madame Poyet had been an excellent audience, attentive and interested, but Imogen and Esmeralda were even better, positively rapt. Richard was slightly less so, being slightly distracted—doubtless by thoughts occasioned by our discussion that morning—but he did not fidget, and there was no sound to disrupt my oratory, save for the muted sputtering of the fire in the hearth and the occasional distant hoot of a barn owl.

Everything went very smoothly until I reached the passage in which Ethelred slays the witch. Forewarning allowed me to make the most of it, in terms of suspense and drama, and I found myself striking a pose as Ethelred prepared to strike the fatal blow, as if I too had a sword in my hand and a mission to fulfil—but when I brought my hand down, Esmeralda screamed, as if I were striking her, and immediately burst into tears.

I stopped reading instantly, and hurried to comfort her—in which action, I noticed, I was alone, for Richard seemed more amused than sympathetic and Imogen was positively frosty, perhaps embarrassed by her sister's weakness.

"But that is wrong!" Esmeralda protested. "The story should not go that way. It is the younger sister, not the older one, with whom the hero should arrange his tryst!"

"You're only saying that because you're a younger sister, and fancy yourself something of a witch!" Imogen retorted, perhaps feeling slightly offended. "No hero should ever make a tryst with any woman but a virtuous one. That goes without saying."

"Saying that something goes without saying, especially when you've just said it, doesn't make it so!" Esmeralda protested.

"Now, now," Richard said. "Don't quarrel, I beg you. It's bad enough when you do by yourselves, or in front of me, but you really mustn't do it in front of a guest. What will my friend think of you?"

That obliged me to insist, loudly and at some length, that I could not and did not think of the sisters in any but the warmest possible terms, and that I considered them both to be perfect young ladies—which seemed to reassure them, although I got the impression that they would both have preferred me to be more selective in my compliments.

"In any case," I concluded, in the hope of restoring Esmeralda's spirits, "we cannot be sure that the witch is irredeemably lost to the story. In fiction, death is not always the end, especially in romances in which magic has a large part to play."

"Do you really think she might return?" Esmeralda asked. "In the flesh, that is, not merely as ghost, like the witch on the roots of whose tragic oak this house now stands?"

"There is no ghost," said Richard, sharply. "I've told you that a hundred times, Smeralda. There are merely shadows in the mist, of sheep and goats and hunting owls." He often shortened Esmeralda's name in that way, although he never used any diminutive of "Imogen", perhaps because of the lack of any ready euphonious substitute.

"And even if there were a ghost," said Imogen, "it would more likely belong to one of the witch's victims than the witch herself."

"But she had no victims!" Esmeralda protested. "She was a virtuous witch, who was unjustly persecuted because she was beautiful, and tempted too many men, in spite of her own faithful desire."

Evidently, I was not the only one that Richard Carstairs had recklessly invited to make up their own tales when solid historical evidence had nothing to say. I began to worry about what I had said, for I had no real reason to believe that the witch might return to Sir Launcelot Canning's story—and I had a dire suspicion that, even if she did, it might well be as a malevolent ghost bent on vengeance...which would not please Esmeralda at all, if her exclamations could be trusted.

I resolved that I would read the rest of the text myself, privately, before risking another public reading, although I doubted that I would be released from my obligation to complete the story for Richard and his sisters, now that I had begun it.

Once again, when I went to bed, I was very tired, partly because Richard and I had walked so far that morning—all the way to Leigh and back—and partly because I had slept so fitfully the previous evening. I had shaken off my aches and pains, and the wine I had drunk at dinner had been topped off with a generous brandy night-cap, so I had the soporific effect of good liquor to assist me as well, but I have to admit that it was with some trepidation that I lay my head on the pillow, for I had had more than enough food for thought to fuel a welter of dreams.

At first, I think, I did sleep soundly, without any disturbance, but eventually, I found myself dreaming. Much of what I dreamed, at first, did not cling to my memory, but I retained vague impressions of witnessing a company of hooded witches chanting to raise a storm, and of joining in the chant myself, as one of their number. That was fleeting, though, and was eventually displaced by a far stranger dream, in which my dream-self went down into the cellar of the house, to find it very different from the appearance it had earlier presented to my waking self. It was empty of ordinary goods, and roots were intruding in abundance through the mortar of the crumbling walls. The floor was moist with sea-water leaked from the tide.

When I tried to get out of the cellar, I could not find a door, and had to go to the hatch through which coal was tipped in order to call for help—but all that I could see outside was mist, with shadows moving therein that were surely not the shadows of sheep, goats or owls. One of them did come toward me in response to my appeals, and I was sure that it was a woman, although I could not identify her by her stature or her figure, and she turned aside when a plaintive voice cried out in the mist, saying: "Don't, Smeralda!"

I stepped back from the hatch, disappointed, and then discovered that the cellar was shrinking—unless I was growing larger—so that its walls pressed in upon me and forced me to curl up like a fetus. Instead of crushing me, however, the walls absorbed me, so that my flesh fused with the body of the house, and my intelligence was distributed throughout its structure, creating a vantage-point from which I could see into every room simultaneously, including the bedrooms of the three siblings who were my hosts. Richard was sleeping peacefully— blissfully, one might almost say—but his two sisters were both restless, each in her own way.

They too were dreaming, and both were dreaming about Ethelred, the hero of *The Mad Trist*, each dreaming within her dream of an eventual meeting at the end of his story.

Imogen was dreaming of an ultimate meeting in a sunlit glade, full of colored flowers, in an atmosphere sweet with perfume, where Ethelred knelt down in order to kiss the hem of her silken dress and implore her to be his bride. She was on the point of acceptance when a shadow fell upon the glade, and the sunlight was replaced by a gentile night, while the colored flowers withered and the perfume was replaced by a noxious odor of putrescence…and then a spectral voice spoke, as if out of chilly mist, saying: "Thou shalt not have him, for he is mine, bought with my blood."

Esmeralda was dreaming of an encounter in the topmost chamber of a tall tower, which was almost filled with a huge bed with silken sheets, in which she lay naked. Ethelred was naked too, and moved toward her lovingly…but at that point, the silken sheets seemed to come to life, and twist themselves into serpentine forms, which coiled around the two would-be lovers before they could secure their embrace, and a spectral voice spoke, as if resonating from the spiral stairway of the tower, saying: "Thou shalt not have him, for he is mine, pledged to me in his dreams."

Then, I tried to withdraw my soul from the house, to separate myself from its strange carcass, and it seemed that I pulled and writhed with all my might, until the very walls stretched and flexed, but I could not get away—and I heard a voice speak, as if from behind me, saying: "Thou art mine, for I have you captive now, and you cannot go until you have raised me from my grave and fulfilled my curse, for which I have been waiting these two hundred and fifty-seven years."

"I will not do it," my dream-self replied. "It is no part of my desire to raise the dead, whether they be wicked or unjustly pursued."

"You have no choice," the voice replied, "for the book possesses you now, and you must read it to the end, final chapter and all."

I should perhaps have woken up at that point, with my heart pounding, but I did not. Instead, I relaxed again, and my dream-self flowed out of the house and into the marsh, expanding into the harsh, salty soil and the rugged vegetation, eventually meeting an advancing tide and dissolving in the sea. It was a slow process, though not an unpleasant one.

I slept peacefully after that, for what seemed like hours, and awoke largely refreshed.

At breakfast, the girls were on their best behavior again,

treating one another with the kind of affection that sisters are supposed to bestow on one another. They reminded Richard of his promise to allow them to accompany us on our morning walk, and he readily agreed. Before we set out, however, the postman arrived, bringing four letters for Richard and—much to my surprise—one for me. My surprise increased when I scrutinized the address on the envelope, and failed to recognize Dupin's handwriting.

For a fleeting moment, I assumed that it must be from Saint-Germain, but when I had opened the envelope and unfolded the single sheet contained within it, I saw that it was signed *Catherine Poyet*. It was dated the nineteenth—the previous day—and written on notepaper baring the heading of Mivart's Hotel in Mayfair.

> *I cannot stop thinking about the story you began to read to me*, it read. *I must know how it ends, even if I can only obtain a synoptic account from your lips, rather than hearing the actual words read aloud. Please meet me in London on the twenty-first. We cannot meet at the hotel, for obvious reasons, so I suggest a rendezvous—a trist, if you like—by Wren's tomb in St. Paul's Cathedral, at noon. There is no need to reply if you agree, but if not, please let me know at the above address, by return of post if possible.*

This struck me as a very odd communication indeed, and my first instinct was to run after the postman and tell him to wait while I composed a hasty reply, making my apologies. I could not move, however; I was nailed to the spot by my own uncertainty and irresolution. In the end, I simply folded up the piece of paper and put it away.

I am indeed "possessed" by the book, I thought, *and it seems that I am not the only one. I am bound for my own mad trist—that much is obvious. But what is there to fear? What can there possibly be to fear?*

I was acutely aware, however, that I still had not the slightest idea whether Sir Launcelot Canning's strange adventure-story had a tragic ending or a happy one…or another kind of ending entirely

CHAPTER SEVEN
The Story Unfolds

I was tempted to leave *The Mad Trist* in the house while we all went out for our walk, but did not dare. Suppose it were to disappear? I would never know, then, how the story ended, and I really could not bear the idea of being stranded in ignorance forever. I kept the volume in my pocket, as had become my invariable habit.

As things transpired, I had no call to bring it out, and the walk progressed very calmly indeed. With Richard present, the two girls were markedly less exuberant and flirtatious than they had been the previous afternoon, and the previous evening's brief embarrassment seemed to have left an imprint on both of them. The dogs were not with us, the groundsman having claimed them to assist him in his duties.

We walked to the ruins of Hadleigh Castle, on the inland side of the ridge rather than the marsh side. When we arrived, Richard gave us a long and tedious account of the history of the edifice, from its erection by Edward III to its being sold for demolition in Tudor times. Richard seemed to take personal offense at the thought that such an interesting edifice could have been broken up for building materials, and there was indignation in his voice as he pointed out the remains of the smelting oven constructed to melt down the lead from the stained-glass windows.

"Why did the demolishers leave those two fragments standing?" Esmeralda asked, pointing to the surviving wall of the old watch-tower and a triangular block of masonry.

"I'm not sure," Richard replied, "but I imagine that it was done deliberately, to construct a kind of architectural ghost—a plaintive relic of the castle that was."

The view over the estuary was a fine one. The Kent marshes, on the far side, extended all the way to the Medway and the port of Chatham, but the ruins of Hadleigh's complementary castle, Queensborough, were clearly visible on their own hill. The crest on which Hadleigh castle stood was an ideal place for flying kites, which some of the local children were gladly doing. Imogen and Esmeralda looked on, both pretending that they were now too old to be interested in such pastimes, but there was a slight hint of envy in Esmeralda's golden-gleaming eyes.

All in all, it was a very peaceful and pleasant morning, whose welcoming normality allowed me to leave the disquieting disturbances of the night far behind, if not to put them out of my mind entirely. We returned home refreshed and thoroughly exercised; our tiredness was pleasant, and not at all insistent, urging us to quiet reflection rather than drowsiness, and the girls seemed to have conquered their competitive spirit for the time being, although that did not stop them showering me with unsubtle flatteries whenever I yielded to their insatiable appetite for more stories about my life and adventures in Paris.

Richard and I spent the afternoon in his study, looking at books and discussing our recent reading; that too seemed very ordinary, and if Richard was not quite as amusing in his erudition as Auguste Dupin, the change of style only added to the relaxation of the occasion.

"I have ever been a night-owl when it comes to reading and writing," I told him, "but that is because Paris is so busy, noisy and odorous by day. If I lived in a haven of peace like this, I believe that I might accustom myself to daylight rather than candlelight, and lose my affection for shadows."

"If you lived here," Richard said, "I'm quite sure that you'd lose your affection for shadows. I don't believe in ghosts, and won't permit the girls to believe in them either, but there's something about the solitude and silence here, and the house's position on a margin between two very different landscapes, that is conducive to fantasy. The sheep glide so silently over the marshland that even I am sometimes taken by surprise in poor light, and my imagination is ever-ready to mistake the calling of curlews for human voices. Sometimes, I wish that I had never heard that silly story regarding the origin of the Lodge's name."

"The stillness of the night does seem to encourage highly-colored dreams," I admitted. "By the way, is there any possibility that we might go to London tomorrow. It's a long drive I know, but...."

He was quick to interrupt me. "Every possibility," he assured me. "It's a good idea, for I have business matters to attend to there, and once that's done, I'd love to show you the Museum library. The girls will object, I dare say, but they've been neglecting their lessons and their chores since you arrived. They'll be perfectly safe in the servants' care, and we can easily get back by nightfall, now that the evenings are getting longer. We'll do it."

Again, we ate relatively early, before retiring to the drawing-room. There was no music that evening, so I proceeded forthwith to read the second instalment of *The Mad Trist*. I knew that I would not quite have time to reach the final chapter—and did not want to do so while I was reading aloud, in any case—but I was sure that I could get close to the climax, given the slenderness of the volume.

To tell the truth, the middle section of the story—which included the three passages quoted by Poe and much routine derring-do besides—was a disappointment to me. It described the various stages of Ethelred's journey, or quest, in terms that were crudely allegorical and somewhat overdressed with gaudy décor. There was far too much gold and silver in it for my liking, credited to objects and edifices that no sane manufacturer or builder would ever have crafted in such unsuitable metals. Ethelred's various combats soon became tedious to me, although the girls—to whom such materials were much less familiar—seemed to enjoy them, especially the dragon-slaying.

I suppose that I was a trifle impatient to get through the journey and arrive at the "trist" itself, and that might have affected my performance, making it a trifle listless. On the other hand, Esmeralda was clearly determined not to make an exhibition of herself again, and was almost feigning indifference, while Imogen was practising her poise and decorum. Even so, when I closed the book, both girls protested.

"Do go on," Imogen begged. "I can see from here that there are only a few pages left, so we can easily finish the story tonight. It's not yet late—the last vestiges of twilight have not yet turned black"

"There are not so very few pages left," I told her, "And I must confess that I'm rather tired. The country air is refreshing, after the reek of Paris and the dust of the roads, and also a trifle intoxicating, but it does make a city-dweller like myself feel rather tired—and your brother and I must make an early start in the morning, if we are to get to London in good time."

That deflected the protest away from the story, as both sisters set about arguing that they ought to be allowed to come with us.

"Richard never takes us to London," Esmeralda said, "for he always has *business* to attend to, and needs to be alone in order to have access to the Museum reading room, where no women are allowed. You could show us the sights, though: the Tower, St. Paul's and the Houses of Parliament."

"That's not possible, Smeralda," Richard cut in. "We both have business to attend to in the morning, and we shall both be going to the reading room in the afternoon. I'll make another trip one day soon, especially to acquaint you with the major features of the city, but it cannot be tomorrow. You must be patient."

"Patient!" cried Esmeralda. "I've been patient all my life. Imogen and I could easily grow old while being patient! We're little more than ghosts ourselves, haunting the border of the marsh. When will our real lives, our flesh and blood lives, actually begin?"

"Soon enough, Smeralda," Imogen chipped in. "For me, at least—after all, I have been granted permission to visit our good friend in Paris, have I not?"

She certainly had not—not, at any rate, on her own—and Richard was almost as quick as Esmeralda and myself to disabuse her of any such notion. We also had to make it plain to one another that neither of us had given any license or encouragement to any such suggestion, with the result that the discussion became more than a trifle confused. Eventually, though, everything calmed down, and the sisters made their way to their bedrooms, dutifully carrying their candles—for the last vestiges of twilight had definitely turned black by then.

"You must forgive the girls," Carstairs said. "They're overexcited. I hadn't realized that your visit would stir them up so. We have so few visitors, you see, and I've neglected to maintain acquaintances in Pitsea and Hadleigh, while absorbed in my own solitary concerns. I've been able to educate them to a reasonable standard, but I can't turn them into eremitic antiquaries, nor would I wish to if I could. If mother were still alive, I suppose she's be busy making arrangements to marry Imogen off, and to rein in Esmeralda's wild streak, but such matters are beyond my scope—I'm not even very good at playing the substitute father. As I told you before, they're out of control, and I have no idea what to do about it. I should have hired a governess, I suppose, or even sent them to school in Westcliff or Chelmsford, but it's too late now. It's all my fault."

"There's no fault involved," I assured him. "You've done everything a loving brother could, and more. They're wonderful girls, and a great credit to you. Yes, they do need to get out into society a little more, now—but it's by no means too late. Take them to London, when you have the chance, so that they might make friends there—and in the fullness of time, bring them both to Paris, where I shall be only too happy to make up a foursome with you, and introduce you to the capital's more savory cultural delights."

"Yes," he said, "I will. I'm glad you came, for you have

provided us all with a very necessary stimulus. Things need to change, and they will."

I took myself off to bed, then, knowing full well that I was going to dream, and that I was bound to dream about the rendezvous arranged for the following noon. I was looking forward to seeing Madame Poyet again, and was delighted to have discovered her first name. The meeting might, I thought, be the beginning of a beautiful friendship, which would inevitably be continued when we had both returned to Paris—but first, I had to read the final chapter of *The Mad Trist*.

Before getting undressed, I went to the window of my room, in order to look out over the marsh and reassure myself that its actual appearance was as different from that in my dream of the previous night as the cellar's was. Obligingly, the night was clear, quite free of deceptive mists; the stars were shining brightly through the gaps in scattered clouds that were hastening northwards on the wings of a brisk wind. Lights were visible on the Kent shore, and a few on the water of the estuary, but none on the land between the house and the shore. There were, however, grey hazy blurs in the darkness—the fleeces of wandering sheep. Awake as I was, though, there was no possibility of mistaking those strange negative shadows for the spirits of the dead.

Oddly enough, I did hear someone squeal: "Don't, Smeralda!"—but it was only Imogen, reacting to some teasing jest that her sister had ventured, before they retired to bed.

I turned away from the window and took off my jacket, having first removed *The Mad Trist* from the pocket, placing it carefully on my pillow to await my pleasure. I completed my evening ritual calmly and methodically, and then joined the coquettishly-poised volume in the bed.

For a moment or two, stretching myself out beneath the quilt and the sheet in my nightshirt, contemplating Jane Anger's little "boke" by the light of the three wax candles on my nightstand, I did wonder about the wisdom of breaking Stephen Coningsby's injunction. To obey it now, however, would surely be a concession to superstition and suggestibility, unworthy of a rational man of my stern stripe. I was a son of the Enlightenment, and it was my definite duty to oppose obsolete credulity with all my mental might—and besides, I was a friend of Edgar Poe, quite familiar with the temptations of the imp of the perverse. How could Coningsby, no matter how unskilled he might be in matters of social intercourse, ever have thought that the injunction he had shouted after the Paris-Boulogne diligence could have any other effect than to make me utterly determined to read the final chapter in question?

So I read it.

As Imogen had observed, there were not very many pages left unread, and it took me less than half an hour.

As I had feared, Ethelred's quest did not have a happy ending, and as I had suggested—somewhat recklessly, it now transpired—the witch's early death within the tale did not prevent her eventual return. Indeed, when Ethelred finally reaches his appointed *rendezvous*, having successfully overcome all his trials, the lady he finds waiting for him is actually two sisters in one, the virtuous one having been unwittingly possessed by the sly spirit of the other. Believing that he is plighting his troth to the former, he actually commits himself covertly to the other.

As in the early phases of the story, the narrative voice offered a clear implication that in making this commitment, Ethelred is complying with his own secret desire—a desire so secret that he is not only unaware of it consciously, but cannot abide the horror of it when the truth is revealed to him. In the concluding action of the story, the tarnished hero recklessly stabs his deceptive lady-love with his sword, intent on sending the dangerous spirit of the witch to hell.

Even that ending could have been interpreted as having a happy element, if the narrative voice had undertaken to explain that dispossessing the virtuous sister of her flesh and her inconvenient possessor had allowed her to ascend to her allotted place in heaven—but that was not what the final paragraphs of the story undertook to do. Instead, Ethelred immediately repents his action, and curses himself for his impetuosity. He realises that he will now be alone forever, and desperate in his isolation, when he might have had the honest and true love, not merely of the virtuous sister, but of the witch as well. He is tempted to fall upon his own blood-stained sword, but cannot do it—not because it would be a sin, but because he feels that he deserves to live on, in misery and desolation, that being his allotted doom for having mistaken his own desire and his own purpose.

"A mad trist indeed," I whispered, as I closed the book and set it down. "Still, at least there is no chance whatsoever that I have been cursed by my reading, for there is no way in the world that I could ever be driven to impetuous murder, even if I were somehow to be convinced that Imogen, or Esmeralda, or Catherine Poyet, were possessed by the spirit of a witch. I am wiser than that. In fact, I am probably strong enough to read any number of forbidden books and emerge psychologically unscathed, even if a weak-headed man like Coningsby—or perhaps even Saint-Germain—might be far more suggestible."

I shut up then, blew out my candles, and went to sleep.

I did dream, and copiously. I dreamed about Catherine Poyet, about Imogen, and about Esmeralda, and there was not a hint of nightmare about my dream, at least until it passed into a later stage, in which I dreamed that I got up from my bed and went once again to my casement, which overlooked the salt marsh behind the house. The marsh was beset by mists now, and there were shades moving in the mist: ghosts *en route* to or from Purgatory, or some other partial destination.

One of them stepped out of the mist, and came to stand beneath my window, on more solid ground. It was the spirit of a woman.

"Thank you," the spirit said to me. "I have been waiting a long time, and had become impatient. You cannot give me back my flesh, but you have set my spirit free. Don't be afraid—I am in your debt, and you have nothing to fear from me. I shall not even trouble your passions or your credulity, for you know as well as I do that this is all a dream, best experienced passionlessly: not only this tale, but this history, and this entire universe. We are but players in the unending tragedy, not its authors, no matter how determinedly we pretend."

"What is your name?" my dream-self asked the shade, curiously.

"Smeralda," she replied. "Smeralda Sutton—but do not expect to find that name inscribed in history, for the subtlest storms obliterate all traces of their own passing."

"Where can I find the *Black Book*?" my dream-self asked.

"Everywhere," she told me. "The beauty of print is its portability and its ubiquity. Notre-Dame de Paris could only stand in one spot, ugly and ill-formed, hoping to be visited, ringing its crazy bells at appointed hours by way of invitation—but you can go inside a book anywhere, at any time, and lose yourself in a world of illusion. Why bother with individual curses, when the entire universe of print is an enchantment of sorts in itself, and a far better one that any petty malefice could devise or develop? But I am free now, and must not tarry—thank you, again, and farewell."

And with that, she disappeared, leaving me to my rest.

Hours passed, I think, before I woke up in truth—and then I had to hurry, in order to fulfil my own appointment with destiny, in the real world.

CHAPTER EIGHT
The Crypt of St. Paul's

The journey to London was smooth and uneventful, but I found myself fretting the whole way, impatient lest I be late for my appointment. Carstairs knew nothing of my rendezvous, of course, but he had several calls to make and readily agreed to meet me on the steps of the Museum at three. I thought that would give me plenty of time to find out how the land lay with Madame Poyet, and, if it seemed appropriate, to arrange another and more leisurely rendezvous at a later date.

One might imagine that a removal from rural Essex to the heart of London would be akin to a return to Paris, and there were certainly features that the two great cities had in common, especially the seething crowds and the everpresent reek of excrement. Contrary to popular belief in Paris, London is not perpetually beset by dense fogs, nor is its sky constantly full of sulfurous industrial fumes, but there is a strange sense in which nothing there has the same color as its Parisian equivalents. Whether that is because the brickwork and stonework making up the buildings, or the various kinds of smoke that have stained them, are distinct in their composition and quality, or whether it has more to do with the angle of sunlight and the texture of the clouds, I do not know—but the point is that as the Essex mail-coach slowed from gallop to a trot as it reached the streets of Whitechapel, I had no sense of returning to my natural environment, but rather an impression of entering an alien world, in which everything was subtly and slyly altered, as if a mask of civilization had been painted over a cunning barbarism.

We disembarked from the coach at the large crossroads where Cornhill intersects Threadneedle Street and several other thoroughfares, and I parted company from Richard in Cheapside, where I lingered briefly in order to let him draw well away before making my way to the cathedral. The open space in front of St. Paul's, at the top of Ludgate Hill, was as crowded as the streets of the financial center, and there were numerous people on the cathedral floor, although the second morning service had finished some while before. The crypt, by contrast, was almost deserted, and seemed very empty indeed given its extraordinary size—it is one of the few crypts in any British of European churches that duplicates the entire footprint of the ground floor of the edifice, chapels and all.

Wren's tomb is at the eastern end of the south aisle, and is surrounded by the mausolea of his kinfolk; it is the most cluttered and shadowy sector of the crypt—the most ideal place in all of London for a secret meeting.

I was five minutes early, and there seemed no be no one there, so I took up a position in front of the tomb, bowed my head in a sufficiently reverent manner, and waited. My heart was pounding in my breast, and my entire body was thrilling with expectation.

Two or three minutes passed, and then I heard a soft footstep behind me. I turned, with a tremulous flutter in my overworked heart—which abruptly disappeared when I found myself face to face with the emaciated figure of Stephen Coningsby, so ill-dressed that he was reminiscent of a scarecrow.

"Thank you for coming," he said, with a slight sneer in his hoarse voice. "I knew that you would."

"*You* sent the letter?" I said, unable as yet to believe it.

"Yes—I hope you'll forgive the subterfuge." He did not sound as if he cared a fig whether I forgave him or not. "It was very easy to track you across the channel, and to obtain elaborate reports of your traveling companions. I considered riding over the marshes to ring the bell at Burnt Oak Lodge, but I had reason to think that I might be unwelcome there, and outnumbered. It seemed more sensible to meet you in Carstairs' absence. You have the book with you, of course—how could you possibly leave it behind? Have you read it?"

"Yes." My reply was automatic; I had been thrown into such confusion that I was not yet able to think clearly

"All of it?"

"Yes."

"A pity. I had entertained some slight hope that, if my letter arrived in time, you might save the last chapter in order to read it in company with the lovely lady. Obviously, you read it at Burnt Oak Lodge—the worst place imaginable, alas—but did you read it aloud, or privately?"

"All but the last chapter aloud," I told him, still too numb with shock to consider telling a lie. "The last chapter privately, by candlelight."

He groaned softly. "Why, oh why wouldn't you listen to me?" he murmured. "Carstairs does not live there alone, does he?"

"No," I confirmed. "He has two sisters, and three servants, all of whom live in."

Coningsby shook his head, pantomiming disappointment and disapproval. "You stupid, stubborn fool," he said. "Do you have any idea what you have done?"

I was recovering my composure by then, and was very confident that I knew exactly what I had done. I had read a book—a mediocre mock-romance—and that was all.

"If I have brought a curse down on my head," I said, negligently, "then I shall face its consequences bravely—but I cannot believe that there is any such thing as a curse that works, other than by means of the suggestibility of its victim. I have been the victim of suggestions induced by experts, and I know that I am strong enough to withstand them. I am in no danger."

"I gathered that you are very insistent in maintaining that delusion," Coningsby retorted, curling his lip in a rudely contemptuous manner. "I truly wish the curse *were* fated to descend upon your head alone, if only to teach you a necessary lesson—but that's not the way it works, alas. Will you give me the book now?"

"Certainly not," I said. "As I have told you before, it is not mine to give—and if it were, I certainly would not give it to you, or sell it to you, even for a king's ransom. Why do you want it, anyhow? You surely cannot believe that it's the great conspiracy's *Black Book*." ·

That surprised him. His eyes narrowed, and his cadaverous, bloodless features took on a slightly jaundiced tint. "What do *you* know about the *Black Book*?" he demanded, curtly.

"I know where it is," I told him.

That surprised him even more. "You're bluffing," he said—all too accurately, alas.

"If you say so. What did you mean when you told me that Saint-Germain had tricked me in giving me the book?"

"I meant that he was doing you a bad turn—worse, in its way, that sticking a dagger in your back. I had followed the book half way across Europe—a direly difficult trail to follow, until it fell into your hands—and you have no idea how much chagrin it caused me to miss it again, by a matter of minutes, when I thought it had reached its destination. The Harmonicist who passed it to his President must surely have expected Saint-German to keep it, and hoard it away, rather than employ it as a weapon in some petty vendetta."

"Don't be ridiculous," I said. "Saint-Germain has no vendetta against me."

"That's none of my business—but the book is. It was written by one of the members of the great conventicle, as an instrument of malice. It needs to be neutralized. The greater part of the print run was seized by Whitgift's agents and burned, but at least a dozen copies escaped. Two are in America, where the injury of which they are capable is muted—spells work best when closest to home—but that leaves ten to work mischief. Burnt Oak Lodge, I fear, is probably as close to home as that particular copy could ever be. It has doubtless been attempting to have itself conveyed there for more than two hundred and fifty years."

"Utter poppycock!" I said. "The flyleaf declares it to be Jane Anger's copy, so it is probably at home right here and now—although I don't know exactly where the churchyard of the old cathedral was located, or where the signs of the Black Bear and Green Dragon were located within it."

Again, I took him by surprise, but he pulled himself together instantly. "So you and Carstairs have put your heads together," he said. "If you imagine that Jane Anger was Joan Orwin or Joan Broome, though, you're mistaken."

"You can't think that she was the Queen!" I protested.

He laughed, but there was no humor at all in the dry cackle. "No, I don't," he said. "I haven't been able to discover her name, or her exact status within the conspiracy, or what became of her—but she certainly wasn't at Court."

"Her name was Smeralda Sutton," I said, on impulse. I was determined to keep on surprising him, until at least an inkling of astonishment took hold.

"How do you know that?" he asked, uncertainly, evidently wondering whether Richard Carstairs had access to some documentary source that had so far evaded him.

"She told me so herself," I reported, "in a dream."

This time, he did not laugh. He was a man who believed in curses, and also in the oracular power of dreams—and I did, after all, have the book in my custody...the book which, if I had been telling the truth and he was correct in his estimations, really had contrived to make its way home, using me as its final instrument.

Unfortunately, Coningsby's patience had worn thin, and he was not to be ensnared with teasing nuggets of antiquarian lore. He reached into his pocket and produced a gun—an antique muzzle-loading duelling-piece.

"Give me the book," he said.

"Don't be ridiculous," I said. "I've been threatened with Colt revolvers—and fired upon, too. You can't possibly imagine that a toy like that can frighten me."

"Whether it can frighten you or not," he retorted, "it can most certainly kill you. I'm not a bad man, and certainly no murderer, but I have a higher duty here than I owe to your miserable, stupid life. Hand over the book, or I'll blow your head off."

He raised his arm, as if he really were taking part in a duel, rising to the challenge and preparing to fire at the drop of a handkerchief—but his thumb had not yet pulled back the weapon's crude hammer, and his finger was not wrapped around the trigger. Indeed, his arm was trembling, and his fingers fumbling as they sought their position. Carstairs was right; he was not a bad man, at heart, and murder went against his grain—but he really was convinced that there was a higher duty at stake here.

I realized, much to my discomfort, that he really was prepared to fire if I did not yield to his threat—and that the solid bulk of Christopher Wren's tomb was behind me, preventing me from backing away.

My heart was pounding again, and I felt cold sweat on my brow—but it never occurred to me to reach into my pocket and surrender the book. I, too, was answerable to a higher duty. I had never realized that I was as brave as I seemed to be at that moment.

A stout cane suddenly descended upon Coningsby's tremulously outstretched arm, whistling through the air with the force of the blow. The cane struck him square upon the wrist, hard enough to crack the bone if not to shatter it, and he cried out in shock and pain.

He dropped the gun, and a shadow moved out of the gloom between the mausolea of Wren's descendants, leaping forward with considerable athleticism to pick it up.

"Now, now, Mr. Coningsby," said the shadow, as it straightened up to reveal itself as a man, seemingly young but probably not as young as he seemed. "This is not the way for a respectable bibliomaniac to behave. You should be ashamed of yourself."

Coningsby was clutching his right wrist in his left hand, and there were tears in his eyes, but he blinked them away, trying to bring his unexpected adversary into focus. "Who the hell are you?" he snarled.

"Auguste Dupin," said the newcomer, with a slight bow, and a brief smile addressed to me. "You really should not boast about the ease with which you followed my friend's trail, when the trail you left in following it was even more prominent. How could you expect that the enquiries you made in Paris would not come to my attention? And how could you not expect that I would react?"

Coningsby tried to reply, but he was gritting his teeth too hard against the throbbing pain of his injury, and could only contrive a sound part-way between a hiss and a grunt.

Dupin turned to me. "I believe you have something for me, my friend," he said, placidly.

Silently, I took *The Mad Trist* out of my pocket, and handed it over.

"Thank you," said Dupin. Then, without further ado, he held the book out to Stephen Coningsby. "There you are, Mr. Coningsby," he said. "Take it, with my compliments—it's yours. Now, was that so hard? Did you really need to go to the trouble of forging a letter from a respectable lady and equipping yourself with a firearm? Why did you not simply come to me?"

Coningsby was flabbergasted—but probably no more so than I was. Again, the scarecrow tried to speak, but managed no more than a strangled stutter.

"What on earth are you doing, Dupin?" I cried, in anguish.

"Come, come," said Dupin. "You know me well enough by now, my friend. Am I the kind of man to hoard a book in my library simply because it is rare, when there is someone else who wants it so much more than I do?"

"But he intends to burn it!" I protested.

"That does seem a shame, if it's true," said Dupin, equably, "but the work is of no great literary value, so far as I know. You've read it—what did you think of the story?"

"Clumsy and implausible," I admitted, but hastened to add: "albeit not uninteresting, in psychological terms. Then again, the volume is an authentic antique, and was once owned by Jane

Anger herself…the pioneering feminist."

"Can you be sure of that?" Dupin asked, mildly. "Anger is not a common English surname, to be sure, but there are likely to have been a good dozen Janes with that surname during the last two hundred and fifty years."

I stared at him helplessly, unable to believe that we could be holding such a discussion in such a situation. I still could not believe that he had simply handed the book over to a man who probably intended to destroy it, without even reading it for himself.

Coningsby was already backing away with his prize, clutching it avidly in his good hand while he let the injured one dangle free. When he thought he had withdrawn to an adequate distance, he turned on his heel and ran, as if all the Devil's earthly minions were after him.

"What have you done, Dupin?" I complained. "That volume is priceless."

"Perhaps," he said, in that irritating way he had of conceding every argument in such a skeptical tone that one always felt that he had not given an inch. "Should I have let him shoot you, then, and pluck it from your pocket while you bled to death?"

"But once you'd disarmed him, either one of us could have knocked him down easily in a fist-fight."

"Which, as I told him, is not the way that respectable biblio-maniacs ought to behave." His tone was gentle, almost conde-scending. "Come on, my friend," he continued, "let's go up into the light. It's gloomy down here, and I'm sure that Christopher Wren and Admiral Nelson would rather rest in peace."

Meekly, I followed him—as I invariably did, whether I understood his actions or not.

CHAPTER NINE

The Meaning of *The Mad Trist*

"I don't understand," I said to Dupin, as we walked westwards down Ludgate Hill in the direction of the Museum. "I don't understand at all."

"What don't you understand?" Dupin asked, a trifle wearily.

"Why did you give the book to Coningsby?"

"Because he wanted it so badly that he was willing to kill to get it."

"But he's completely out of his mind!"

"Perhaps—but that doesn't alter the fact. He believes the book to be cursed, and powerfully so. He believes that the concentrated power of an entire conventicle of witches, flushed with the power of believing that they had raised a storm to destroy the Spanish Armada, was channelled into the curse in question."

"That's nonsense!" I protested. "His antiquarian obsession has addled his brain."

"It *is* nonsense," Dupin agreed. "I'm by no means convinced that the conventicle did curse the book, although I'm willing to believe that some such conspiracy might well have existed, and might well have attempted some such experiment. Even if they did, curses are impotent in a strictly literal sense—but as every would-be magician knows, there is no strict division between the magical and the psychological. Curses can be effective, even in the absence of any explicit causality, and whether people believe in them consciously or not. Often, the mere suggestion is sufficient to cause trouble, if not before tragedy strikes, then afterwards. Saint-Germain knows that very well."

We did not go straight on into Fleet Street but turned right in order to head in the general direction of Holborn, although we would have to pass through a labyrinthine series of side-streets in order to get there.

"Coningsby said that Saint-Germain had tricked me," I told Dupin, "but I could not see how he had done so or why he would want to."

"That is because you underestimate both his subtlety and his malice. Do you remember what he said on the occasion when you met him for the first time?"

"Every word. Which remark did you have in mind?"

"When I still thought, erroneously, that he might be the chief villain of that particular piece, and Mademoiselle Valdemar his innocent victim, I told him that if he hurt a hair on her head, I would reckon with him, and he, being very annoyed—perhaps not entirely without justification—told me that if I hurt her, *he* would reckon with *me*. You have assumed that, because he played a hand in the trick with the Chinese lanterns, he had forgotten that threat. I always knew that he had not, and that it would only be a matter of time before he sought a reckoning, by inflicting a punishment that he deemed to fit the crime. That is why he took the opportunity to procure the copy of *The Mad Trist* for which Mr. Coningsby was hunting high and low."

"But why did he give it to me rather than conveying it directly to you?"

"Again, his twisted notion of poetic justice. In his eyes, I injured him by damaging his protégée, so he set out to damage… well, the nearest thing to a protégé that he imagined me to have. If you had managed to pass the book on to me without sustaining any harm, he would still have had a further opportunity to play his game—but he must have been confident that Coningsby would catch up with you eventually, and explain the curse to you, even if he could not plant a sufficient seed of suspicion before you even left Paris."

"That he did," I conceded. "My ingenuity, combined with Richard's, was easily equal to the task of uncovering a tangled web of rumor and suspicion, which not only reached out to embrace Burnt Oak Lodge but a fellow-passenger on the Boulogne-to-Folkestone ferry. It was all in my mind, of course...but my mind has ever been active, especially when I sleep."

"You have had more bad dreams, then?" Dupin asked, rhetorically. "Saint-Germain knew of that propensity, remember, thanks to Mademoiselle Valdemar's little joke. Saint-Germain will certainly say, if you accuse him of evil intent, that this business too was merely a joke—a subtle mind game, of a sort calculated to amuse and flatter intelligent men rather than hurt them."

"But you didn't want to receive his gift," I observed, thoughtfully. "Not because you believe that you might have been accursed had you hung on to it for more than a minute, but because you didn't want to play his game."

"I didn't want to play his game," Dupin confirmed—which was, I suppose, better than saying *perhaps*, although it struck me as a rather unspecific reply, if not frankly evasive.

For once, I pressed him. "Come on, Dupin," I said. "You're playing games yourself. Do you or do you not believe that there might have been some danger in accepting that book and placing it on your shelves?"

"Only in the sense that Coningsby was prepared to go to any lengths to retrieve it. As you know, I already have several books on my shelves that are reckoned direly dangerous—but none has yet proved fatal, to me or anyone else."

"So you don't believe that I'm in any danger, as a result of having had it about my person for several days, and having read it from beginning to end?"

"Time will tell," he replied, far less reassuringly than I could have hoped. "But this interrogation is a little one-sided, don't you think? May I ask you a question?"

"Of course," I said. "Do you want to know the story told in

The Mad Trist, and how it ends?"

"That too," he said, "But first, what did you mean when you told Coningsby that you know where the *Black Book* is?"

"Ah!" I replied, slightly discomfited as well as surprised that he should pick up that particular point. "I was being provocative—but I did have a dream last night, which included a brief dialogue between myself and the hypothetical witch of Burnt Oak Lodge—who was, in my soaring flight of fancy, the member of the great conventicle who used the pseudonyms Jane Anger and Sir Launcelot Canning. She told me that her name was Smeralda Sutton, and when I asked her, sarcastically, where the *Black Book* was, she replied 'Everywhere.' It was only a dream, of course, but…well, the answer stuck in my memory, as these things sometimes do."

"Indeed—and in our dreams, we are sometimes capable of insights that our waking minds struggle in vain to grasp."

"What do you mean?" Just for an instant, I felt a thrill of fear. I had no intention, of course, of telling him the whole substance of the previous night's dream, or the dreams I had experienced on the preceding nights.

"You are probably some way ahead of me in plumbing the depths of the mystery of the so-called great conspiracy," Dupin continued, relaxing into his loquacious mode, "but tracking Coningsby and his obsession has given me to believe that he is particularly preoccupied with the conspiracy's supposed desire to harness the innate magic of print to its own ends—a venturesome ambition, compared with which the conjuring of lethal storms at sea might be reckoned child's play. Perhaps more importantly, it was an unnecessary ambition, since the magic of print was already working to their ends."

"Satanic ends?" I queried.

"In a metaphorical fashion, perhaps. But the members of the conventicle, even though I cannot believe that it included such persons as John Dee and Reginald Scot, and was very probably comprised solely of women of Jane Anger's subversive stripe, cannot possibly have seen themselves as Satan's slaves. They must have considered themselves to be an *avant garde* of the New Learning, in quest of alchemical secrets. It was not Satan's cause that they wished to advance, even by cultivating the art of inflicting curses, but the cause of women's freedom, and the freedom of the collective soul of humankind. They certainly sought power, but not to do evil for evil's sake…although they might have mistaken the very nature of power, and neglected the danger of unintended consequences."

"Stop talking in riddles, Dupin, I implore you. Say what you mean."

"Very well. Print *does* have a particular power over the human mind, which handwriting does not have. Joan Orwin and Joan Broome, who were among the first generation of dealers in print to make a real effort to woo their customers, and thus to explore the art and craft of seducing readers, were presumably among the first people to figure that out, perhaps because they did not take the printing press as much for granted as their husbands and male competitors.

"The alphabet was invented to provide signs representing the sounds of speech—to make speech concrete and preservable. Early writing was designed to be read aloud, or at least pronounced within the mind of a reader as if it were being heard. Handwriting had to be interpreted that way, because it is idiosyncratic –but print unifies the shapes of letters, and hence the shapes of words. Print thus opens up the possibility of omitting the intermediary stage of real or imaginary pronunciation, and translating the signs on the page directly into meaning. For that reason, as you are well aware, it is possible to read a printed text silently much more rapidly than it could be read aloud— although most literary texts in Elizabethan times, comprising poetry or plays, were still expressly designed to be translated into speech.

"That direct translation of print into meaning, when it occurs, tacitly changes the standpoint of readers, who are no longer forced to serve as mere listeners, outside of a text that is merely being related to them. It opens up the possibility of drawing a reader into the text, as if he were participating in the story... usually by placing himself imaginatively in the protagonist's shoes, and experiencing a character's exploits as if they were his own. The history of literature since the invention of printing has been, in large measure, the development of narrative techniques designed to facilitate that kind of absorption in prose fiction."

"But that's not magic!" I protested.

"Is it not? Objectively, perhaps not—it certainly involves no breach in natural law—but subjectively...do you not feel, when you read a cleverly-crafted *roman* by Monsieur Hugo or Monsieur Balzac, that something magical is happening? Do you not feel that you are entering into the text as if into a world within it—that you have surrendered yourself to the dictates of the author and the momentum of his story, as to the conjurations of a wizard and the authority of his spell?"

"Metaphorically...." I began.

"Metaphorically, of course—and yet, in a compelling manner. Great writers know that they are not wizards, in any but a metaphorical sense—but they feel their power neverthe-less, and may well become subject to similar obsessions. You have seen Monsieur Balzac in dire straits, so you know exactly what I mean. You know full well that books have the power to alter the minds and transform the souls of their readers. To you, not only as a rational man but as a man who is so completely and utterly familiar with the process I am describing, that process does not seem to you to be magical at all...but try to put your-self in the shoes of the Widow Orwin, or the Widow Broome, or the mysterious author who signed herself Jane Anger. To them, all this was new, and they already thought of themselves as witches. How could they not believe that they were, in truth, magicians, if they really had tried to summon a storm to destroy the Armada, once such a storm had actually blown up?"

"That's what you meant about curses working afterwards, if not before," I said, pleased with myself for having remembered. "If you attempt to cast a spell, and the desired event then occurs, how can you not believe that there must have been a causal connection, even if, in fact, it was mere coincidence? That is why poseurs like Saint-Germain and Mademoiselle Valdemar eventually fall prey to their own patter...every successful outcome of their improvised spells serves to convince them, gradually, that they really do have power...even if they knew full well beforehand that their performance was pure invention, or psychological trickery."

"Exactly," said Dupin, with uncharacteristic precision. We had reached High Holborn now, and were not very far from the Museum. We had slowed our pace to a very leisurely stroll, because we were ahead of time.

"And that," I said, to prove that I was now fully in the swim of his argument, "is why the author of *The Mad Trist* believed that she—or perhaps he, if Sir Launcelot really was a man—could produce a book capable of inflicting a curse, if only the narrative could muster sufficient compulsion?"

It was too much to hope that he would continue in a definite vein. "Probably," he said. "But I have a suspicion that Coningsby and Saint-Germain might be barking up the wrong tree, in that respect...and that the author of the book might have made an error. Will you summarize the story for me now? I only have a vague idea of its nature, derived from Poe's citations."

I paraphrased the story as best I could, and added: "But I must say that it is not a particularly engaging work. If the reader really is meant to identify closely with Ethelred, experiencing his adventure as if it were his own...well, all I can say is that Smeralda Sutton was no George Sand, let alone an Alexandre Dumas."

"No," said Dupin. "We could hardly expect an Elizabethan writer, who had never read a novel in her life, to obtain an instant mastery of techniques that would require a further two hundred and fifty years of development."

"Nor can I see how the narrative is designed so as to inflict a curse, however ineptly," I added. "Like many other romances, it is a tale of tragic love, albeit a slightly unusual one."

"That, I suspect, is the whole point," said Dupin.

"You're talking in riddles again."

"I'm sorry. What I mean is that there are two types of magic in which witches were traditionally involved, if the lore of legend and folklore can be trusted. Casting curses was one, but the other was the manufacture of love potions. Alas, the two are not entirely distinct."

I remembered what I had said to Madame Poyet, while in a pedagogical mood myself, about love once having been regarded as a kind of divine madness: an affliction threatening social order, or, in other words, a curse. I had asked her to remember Tristan and Iseult...and she had offered the further example of Claude Frollo and Esmeralda.

"You think that *The Mad Trist* was designed to make its readers *fall in love*," I said, wishing that I could make the suggestion seem more absurd than it actually did, so far as I was concerned...although "fall in love" was more than a trifle euphemistic, in the context of the dreams that I had entertained since first opening the volume.

"I think there is a sense in which a great many prose narratives are designed to encourage people to love, and to direct that love into appropriate channels. From the first Medieval romance to the latest novel by George Sand, that has been a crucial agenda of ambitious fiction. Indeed, I would go so far as to say that our modern obsession with the idea of romantic love, and our modern conviction that love makes a better basis for marriage than economic interest, owe their force almost entirely to the metaphorical magic of fiction...a force that first began to gather strength in the poetry and drama of the Elizabethan court, but gained considerably in impetus from the added potential of print and the development of the novel."

"You amaze me, Dupin," was all I could think of to say... although I was by no means as amazed as I would have liked to pretend.

"What the author of *The Mad Trist* was trying to do, if I am interpreting your synopsis correctly, was to manipulate the affective power of tragedy, which he or she had already savored in dozens of Medieval romances. In fusing the characters of the virtuous sister and the witch, the text was presumably attempting to make a point about the ambiguity of female nature, but the real purpose of the ending, I suspect, was an attempt to make the reader strike an attitude with respect to Ethelred…to make the reader experience the futility of the gesture that Ethelred feels compelled to make, in order to be true to his misconceived ideals. In crude terms, the ending that you have described must have been intended to infuse the reader with the conviction that loving a witch, or a woman less than wholly virtuous, is not wrong—and that slaying such a woman in the name of moral propriety, or in response to a shameful horror of one's own feelings, is a stupid and terrible thing to do, which can only lead to unhappiness and despair…but even if the author intended that crudity, the effect could not be so simple, by virtue of the essential paradoxicality of the power of print."

"Which is?" I queried.

"Come now," said Dupin. "You're only pretending to be naïve. You're following my argument better than you're now willing to admit, although you were proud of it only a few minutes ago. You know full well that texts have subtexts, and that their theses generate antitheses, whether their authors intend them or not. The tragedy of Tristan and Iseult is ostensibly shaped as counsel against the recklessness of falling in love with inappropriate objects of desire, or at least of acting on the desire in question, but hardly anyone takes that lesson from it, at least in modern times. Modern readers sympathize wholeheartedly with Tristan, and think him all the more noble because the compulsion of his infatuation leads him to death. If the author of *The Mad Trist* intended her readers to regret what Ethelred had done, because he regretted it so forcefully and because it left him so utterly desolate, she might have missed her mark, at least with some of them. Some, witnessing and perhaps sharing vicariously in his desolation, might think his plight a price worth paying for having done the right thing, and sacrificing his corrupted fiancée. If the author of *The Mad Trist* really was the author of

Jane Anger's tract in defence of women, and a professed witch to boot, she must have been aware of the effects of that kind of hypocritical delusion...and when she had added a flourish to the last line of her manuscript, before handing it to the printer, she must have suffered a pang of anxiety herself, lest her love potion misfire."

"Nothing is ever simple in your mind, is it, Dupin?" I said, slightly annoyed by his criticism.

"Nothing is ever simple," he told me. "Not, at least, when it is subjected to proper rational analysis. Even the transactions of matter are far more complex than tradition had led us to believe—and the transactions of the human mind are more complicated by a further order of magnitude."

I could not deny that. In any case, we had reached the pillars fronting the British Museum in spite of our snail-like pace. Richard Carstairs was leaning negligently on the one to the right of the door, waiting for me—even though I was not yet late for our appointment.

Richard seemed less than delighted to see Dupin, but greeted him courteously and immediately extended an invitation to him to join us at Burnt Oak Lodge—an invitation that Dupin accepted very graciously. After that, we spent several hours in and out of the Reading Room—the alternation required by the rule of silence, which compelled us to compare notes and hold discussions elsewhere.

I felt quite relaxed, thinking that the whole business with Coningsby and the book had been resolved, and that everything had now been explained, to the limit of rational possibility. None of us, of course, had the slightest inkling of what awaited us back at Burnt Oak Lodge.

CHAPTER TEN
Tragedy and its Subtexts

The journey back to Essex was reasonably comfortable until we got to Pitsea, when three of us had to squeeze on to the bench of Richard's fly. Our inconvenience was, of course, supplemented by that of the horse. Dupin is no featherweight, and he added considerably to the burden pressing on the wheels of the little vehicle, which the nag had to tow along the ill-made roads. Even so, as Richard had promised, we made it back to Burnt Oak Lodge before nightfall, while the last red rays of the setting sun were still shining on our backs, and reflecting from the windows of the house with a suggestion of infernal fire.

The house was in turmoil. The servants rushed out to intercept us, to tell us that Esmeralda had drowned in the lake that morning, and that Imogen was keeping vigil beside her corpse, so distraught that she was on the brink of madness herself.

Richard rushed in to see for himself, and to comfort his surviving sister, while Dupin and I hung back, to question the servants and to ascertain exactly what had occurred.

Apparently, Imogen had decided to go swimming—partly, perhaps in a spirit of competition with her sister, because swimming was something she had mastered, while Esmeralda had not. For that very reason, however, Esmeralda had been determined join her, in order to practise her own skill and perhaps to catch up with her elder sister in at least one accomplishment.

At first, Imogen had protested loudly, calling: "Don't, Smeralda!"—a cry that had attracted the attention of the groundsman, who was on the landward side of the ridge with the two collies, retrieving a stray goat. Esmeralda had seemed, however, in the course of her initial splashing, to be getting the hang of making progress through the water in a controlled and artful fashion, and the groundsman knew that the lake was shallow. Imogen had relaxed her anxiety.

Esmeralda, delighting in her achievement, had drawn away from her sister, giggling—until her foot hand become entangled in fronds of submerged algae, and she had suddenly fallen prey to panic. She could have simply stood on the lake-bed, with her head out of the water, while the others did what was necessary to free her, but she did not have the presence of mind to do that. Instead, she had continued thrashing about, trying—quite unnecessarily—to scream for help.

Imogen, of course, had done everything she could to help, surging forward and trying desperately to free her sister from the treacherous weed. The groundsman had joined in too, armed with his skinning-knife—but by the time that Esmeralda had been cut free, she had taken a great deal of water into her lungs, and all their efforts to make her spew it out again came to naught. The younger sister died as she lay on the bank, unable to draw breath, still helpless to save herself.

According to the story that Dupin skillfully extracted from the distraught servants, it seemed that Imogen now held herself doubly responsible for her sister's death—firstly for having tacitly goaded her by deciding to go swimming, knowing that it would excite Esmeralda's envy, and secondly for having failed to free her from the weed in time to save her life. Richard's absence, and the necessity of having to explain to him what had happened when he returned, had added considerably to her anguish, for the suspicion that he would blame her had added a further burden to her own feelings of guilt.

Richard, of course, did no such thing. Although grief-stricken, he did his utmost, from the very beginning, to persuade Imogen that she had not the slightest reason to feel responsible, and that the whole affair was an unavoidable accident of fate, like the deaths of their father and mother.

It is, alas, not always the case that a trouble shared is a trouble halved, and it did not seem that their partnership in grief assisted Richard or Imogen to feel the horror and pain of what had happened any less. I wish that I could say that my presence, or Dupin's, lent the slightest assistance to the alleviation of their plight, but I could not see any such effect. Indeed, the fact that their grief was witnessed by outsiders, even by a friend as dear as me, seemed to add an extra thorn to their crown of torment.

Eventually, we put Imogen to bed in her own room, and persuaded her to take a draught of laudanum, but Richard could not be subjected to similar merciful treatment. He was restless and raving—and he, like Imogen, made every attempt to blame himself for his sister's misfortune. He should not have gone to London; he should have taken more care to teach her to swim; he should have made more effort to quash the burgeoning sibling rivalry between the two girls. Those supposed errors he voiced, but even in the extremes of grief, he did not go so far as to add that he should not have invited me to stay at Burnt Oak Lodge, thus adding an extra provocative presence to the rivalry in question, or that he should never have let me read to them from *The Mad Trist*, whose tale of two combative sisters was bound to inflame that provocative presence further.

For my own part, I knew that I had to maintain a level head if I were to be of any help at all. It was my duty, as well as my natural inclination, to put all thoughts of blame firmly to one side, including those that might accuse myself. I had committed no fault at all, either in coming to the Lodge, or in reading from the book, or in letting Imogen and Esmeralda into my dreams. I did not need Dupin to explain to me that curses had no power to determine the course of events, or that *The Mad Trist* was not, in any case, cursed with any other power than that possessed by all romances, to laud and channel the impulses of human love. I knew, beyond a shadow of a doubt, that I was not the one who had brought misfortune to Burnt Oak Lodge, any more than the hypothetical witch hanged from the tree on whose long-dead roots the house now balanced had done so from beyond the grave.

Indeed, I was convinced that, had Smeralda Sutton been real, she would have saved her namesake rather than dragging her down to her death. Alas, she was merely a product of my runaway imagination, and had no such power.

When Imogen woke up the next morning Richard went to her bedside in order to comfort her, and presumably had some success. When he emerged, he told me that she had asked to see me. I went immediately.

I sat down by her bedside, in an armchair still warm from Richard's occupancy.

"You will be better soon," I assured her. "This is an inordinately hard blow to bear, but we must withstand such tests, if we are to live bravely and well."

She gripped my hand, and squeezed it. "May I still come to Paris?" she asked.

"Of course," I said. "You and Richard must both come, when your mourning is over. The change of scene will do you good."

"And you will show me the sights?"

"I will."

Her grip relaxed slightly. "I feared that you might not want to," she said, sounding younger than her years. "I feared that it was Smeralda you liked best, Smeralda who had enchanted you, even though I was the older, the one more nearly a woman."

I tried to withdraw my hand, but her grip tightened again, and she looked at me very intently. Although the sun was not yet high in the sky, and her window did not face eastwards, there was a strange gleam in her eyes: a golden gleam, whose like I had only seen once before.

"You should not talk about such things," I said, uneasily. "There never was any need for you and your sister to compete for my attention. I liked you both equally—as if you were my own sisters as well as Richard's."

"But there is only one of us left, now," she said, her eyes full of tears. I could not read the exact quality of the emotion in her voice, and did not really want to try. I could no longer meet her gaze, because I feared that, if I did, I might fall prey to the illusion that Esmeralda was somehow possessing her sister's distraught flesh, injecting her own fervor into Imogen's blood— and that she was desperate to make the most of one last chance to compete for and claim my attention, my affection, and my promise.

I knew that it was nonsense—that the golden fever burning in Imogen's eyes was merely the heat of her grief and anxiety— but I knew too much, by now, about the logic of curses, and about the cunning manner in which they might grip an unbeliever after an event, even more securely than before. I was determined to resist magic of any sort, actual or metaphorical. There was no way on earth that I could allow poor Esmeralda to call to me from beyond the grave, for any purpose whatsoever.

Recalling my conversation with Dupin as we walked through London's busy streets, I told myself that Imogen had read too many novels, without having the experience of life necessary to put their seductive appeal in its proper perspective.

"You must rest now," I told her. "You must be quiet, and calm, and you must not surrender to the sinister effects of dreams and delusions. You must be good, for Richard's sake as well as your own. You must be an adult now, for his sake as well as your own. You must concentrate your mind on the real facts of life, and avoid dangerous fancies. It is your duty to live, and it is what your sister would have wanted. You must be calm, and rational."

"But I may come to Paris, may I not?" she leaded. "In time."

"In time," I assured her. "In time, all things will be possible." I did not know then, and do not know now, why I should have felt like a liar and a hypocrite as I pronounced those words. They should have been true.

The words had their effect, though. She took what I said to heart, and soon recovered from her dangerous anguish—to the extent that she was able to comfort Richard in his grief. That was perhaps as well, for it was a task to which I was ill-fitted.

My own trials were not quite over, though. When I slept, *she* came to me in my dreams, in her own strange fashion. I suppose I should be grateful that she came tenderly, with love in her golden-tinted eyes; I do not think that I could have borne it had she come to accuse me of bringing about her death with a carelessly-imported curse. Even as things were, there were difficulties....

Dupin and I stayed for the funeral, which was held in a village church a mile away, where Esmeralda was buried in the church-yard, in the shade of a yew. We did not prolong our visit there-after, however, as the time did not seem right for antiquarian discussions and the comparison of scholarly ideas.

Richard did not seem sorry to see us go, although Imogen certainly was—and Richard's promise to bring Imogen to visit Paris before the end of the year seemed a trifle hollow to me.

On the ferry from Folkestone to Boulogne I said to Dupin: "If Saint-Germain hears about this tragedy, he might think himself to blame for it, might he not? Having tried to put a curse on me, he will not be able to believe—at least not wholeheartedly—that the curse was not partly responsible for Esmeralda's death."

"I fear so," Dupin replied. "The incident might add one more item to the catalogue of his conversion to credulity—but that is not our fault. We did what we could."

"We are possessed of stronger minds than his and Coningsby's, are we not?" I said. "We can bear the weight of coincidence, without going in quest of non-existent causes."

"The human mind is predisposed to seek patterns," he observed. "From the chaos of events, attentiveness is always avid to find evidence of order, and often takes aboard the false along with the true. Even the strongest mind resists the tempta-tion with difficulty, especially when it relaxes. Have you had more bad dreams these last few nights, my friend?"

"No," I lied. There was no way in the world that I dared tell him that I dreamed almost every night about Imogen, and not merely about Imogen, but about Imogen possessed by Esmeralda's spirit, so that it was really Esmeralda who was seeking me out—and that I had more than once been so horrified by my own reaction to her uncanny presence that my dream-self had had to fight an impulse to stab her in the breast. I did not want him to think me so weak-spirited as to be unable to resist the insidious pressure of *The Mad Trist*, even though I knew any such effect to be mere folly. I did not want to think that of myself, either.

In time, though, the dreams died away. By the time that the real Imogen had put aside her mourning-dress, the Esmeralda-possessed Imogen of my dreams had modestly retired to the shadows, not to be replaced with any other disturbing image.

Imogen never did contrive to visit Paris. She died later that summer, of marsh fever.

Richard did not come to Paris either. I never saw him again, although he did not die for several more years. His death was credited to marsh fever too, in the parish record, but that is because parish records do not recognize such causes as a broken heart. He never completed the book he had planned to write on the history of his neighborhood.

Burnt Oak Lodge still stands, I believe, but it has been empty for some time. Its flocks no longer roam the marsh by day or by night...the gentile night is empty now, even of ghosts.

Two years after that fateful meeting in St. Paul's crypt, Stephen Coningsby was killed in a duel with a rival collector, over a book that each of them accused the other of stealing from him. According to rumor, Coningsby's arm shook so much that he missed his shot entirely, but his opponent was made of sterner stuff. I never knew for certain what he had done with Jane Anger's copy of *The Mad Trist*, but I cannot believe that he burned it; he was, after all, a bibliomaniac, and exactly the kind of man to hoard a book in his library simply because it was rare.

I never saw Catherine Poyet again, in London or in Paris. Although she kindly sent me several invitations by post, soliciting my presence at one of her occasional salons, I always sent my apologies. Nor did I ever dream about her again, having put such inconvenient temptations firmly and finally behind me.

As for the self-styled Comte de Saint-Germain, more will require to be said of his future and fate in further episodes in these memoirs, and I shall leave more explicit comment until then.

Looking back over those last few paragraphs, I am reminded once again of Dupin's observation that the human mind is predisposed to see patterns, questing for causal patterns where none exist, or ever could exist. So many terrible and tragic things happen in the world, on a daily basis, that it is far too easy, in retrospect, to find supposed evidence of curses and maledictions, and strangely difficult even for strong minds to resist the temptation—but we must resist it, if we are ever to secure the victory of heroic reason over superstitious dread.

Mercifully, I can at least be sure of one thing: I have had a copy of *The Mad Trist* in my possession for several days, and have read it from cover to cover, without any curse coming down upon my head. I have suffered no injury or misfortune, and can say with utter conviction that if the story was intended as some eccentric sort of love potion, it did not work on me— not for very long, at least. I am, it seems, once again immune to such feverish afflictions. Like my good friend Auguste Dupin, I remain triumphantly undamaged by all the wiles of all the magicians in Paris.

Smeralda Sutton was wrong; the *Black Book* is not quite everywhere; there are still corners of the collective soul of mankind that it cannot reach.

ABOUT THE AUTHOR

Brian Stableford was born in Yorkshire in 1948. He taught at the University of Reading for several years, but is now a full-time writer. He has written many science-fiction and fantasy novels, including *The Empire of Fear*, *The Werewolves of London*, *Year Zero*, *The Curse of the Coral Bride*, *The Stones of Camelot*, and *Prelude to Eternity*. Collections of his short stories include a long series of *Tales of the Biotech Revolution*, and such idiosyncratic items as *Sheena and Other Gothic Tales* and *The Innsmouth Heritage and Other Sequels*. He has written numerous nonfiction books, including *Scientific Romance in Britain, 1890-1950*; *Glorious Perversity: The Decline and Fall of Literary Decadence*; *Science Fact and Science Fiction: An Encyclopedia*; and *The Devil's Party: A Brief History of Satanic Abuse*. He has contributed hundreds of biographical and critical articles to reference books, and has also translated numerous novels from the French language, including books by Paul Féval, Albert Robida, Maurice Renard, and J. H. Rosny the Elder.

VALDEMAR'S DAUGHTER

Following the sad demise of Ernest Valdemar, as related in the story by Edgar Allan Poe, his mortal remains are dispatched to his daughter in Paris—but they do not arrive on schedule, and the Chevalier Auguste Dupin is forced to play detective yet again in tracking them down.

The mesmerists of the Philosophical Harmonic Society of Paris seem to be implicated in the mystery, most especially the society's enigmatic President, the Comte de Saint-Germain. In the meantime, Honoré de Balzac lies at death's door, convinced that only the magic of Valdemar's remains can save him. Dupin must race to solve the puzzle, if the great writer's life is to be saved. Will he thwart his adversary in the nick of time?

Borgo Press Fiction by BRIAN STABLEFORD

VALDEMAR'S DAUGHTER

A ROMANCE OF MESMERISM

BRIAN STABLEFORD

THE BORGO PRESS

MMX

VALDEMAR'S DAUGHTER

DEDICATION

For Monica,

Forty Years On

CONTENTS

"As I rapidly made the mesmeric passes, amid ejaculations of "Dead! dead!" absolutely bursting from the tongue and not from the lips of the sufferer, his whole frame at once, within the space of a single minute, or less, shrunk, crumbled, absolutely rotted away beneath my hands. Upon the bed, before that whole company, there lay a nearly liquid mass of loathsome, of detestable putrescence."

Edgar Poe, "The Facts in the Case of M. Valdemar" (1845)

"Magnetism and the magnetic effects that result from it prove, for all men of intelligence, the existence of a new science different from that of the old schools. In effect, one may characterize this dissemblance by saying that the knowledge that forms the assemblage of official science represents dead nature; the other, on the contrary, is the true science of life. They are separated by nuances so trenchant that it is impossible to confuse them."

M. le Baron du Potet, *La Magie dévoilée* (1852)

"Because the very elixir that pours a more glorious life into the frame, so sharpens the senses that these larvae of the air become to thee audible and apparent; so that, unless trained by degrees to endure the phantoms and subdue their malice, a life thus gifted would be the most awful doom a man could bring upon himself."

Edward Bulwer-Lytton, *Zanoni* (1842)

CHAPTER ONE

A N o c t u r n a l V i s i t o r

One of the strangest affairs in which my long-distance relationship with my American correspondent ever involved me—
and with which my great friend Auguste Dupin was able to
render invaluable assistance—was that of the mortal remains
of the late Ernest Valdemar. Naturally, I sent a detailed report
of the whole affair to my correspondent, but he was unable
make any use of it in his work, because public pressure had
already compelled him to adopt a defensive stance, asserting
vigorously—but falsely, of course—that the carefully-abridged
account of Valdemar's last days he had published in December
1845 was purely a hoax. Whether it would have been dangerous
for him to assert otherwise, and from what quarter the danger
might have come, I cannot say. Nor, for that matter, can I say
with any absolute certainty that his silence protected him,
for the exact circumstances of his death in 1849 remain stubbornly mysterious—as, I suppose, do the exact circumstances
of Honoré de Balzac's death in the following year.

I had no advance warning of the fact that my correspondent
had recommended anyone to send me a consignment, or by what
means, so I was taken entirely by surprise by the events that
unfolded with such uncanny rapidity in the month of February
1846, not long after the Cracow rising had plunged Poland into
chaos. Paris seemed still to be deep in the hibernation of a cruel
winter, not yet able to stir itself properly, even though the ice
and snow had largely disappeared, leaving only a slight dusting

of night frost to turn the city silver by night.

Dupin arrived at my door shortly after nine, as was his frequent habit in those days, even when the weather was fierce, and we settled down in my sitting-room to discuss matters literary and philosophical. Although I had a decanter of brandy warming on the mantelpiece I had also prepared a jug of mulled wine, as I routinely did when the weather was exceptionally cold—I had done so every time I had anticipated his visit since the end of December—and my invariable suggestion that we start the evening with the libation in question was gratefully accepted.

"This is not your usual recipe," he observed, having taken a few sips. "You have been experimenting again." There was no hint of accusation in his tone; apparently, he approved of the taste and the texture of the combination of spices that I had mixed with the red wine. I did not tell him that I could claim no credit for the experiment in question, because the combination had been made up for me by the local herbalist-cum-apothecary.

Dupin settled into his armchair with his glass and took off his boots in order to warm his stockinged feet on the edge of the fireplace; evidently, he was glad of an opportunity to relax, and for once, our conversation was a trifle lacking in energy. Although we had left the most intense period of winter dark-ness behind, spring still seemed a distant prospect, and we both seemed to be suffering from the kind of affective disorder that makes so many residents of Paris seem sluggish once Mardi Gras has passed and Lent has established its dour empery over the public mood. I think we were both half-asleep by midnight, although that was an hour when, night-owls as we were, our wits usually came more fully to life. It was with a certain annoyance that I was snatched out of my reverie half an hour later when I heard my doorbell ring.

I cannot say that I was unduly surprised by the fact itself, in spite of the unsociable hour and chilly weather, for the sad truth is that the peaceful initial period of our initial acquaintance, when Dupin had consented to share my rented accommoda-

tion for a while, was decisively past. Dupin's reluctant celebrity had spread considerably further than the Prefecture by that date. Although he had moved back to his own apartment some time before, only visiting the house that we had once shared when the mood took him, anyone who came looking for him by night knew well enough where to enquire for him if he was not at home. I *was* surprised, however, when I answered the door—personally, for I kept no concierge or valet—to find that the caller was a woman, and doubly surprised when she asked for me rather than my friend.

When I had confirmed my identity, I thought for a moment that she might throw herself upon me, although she controlled herself, and contented herself with saying, in a rather plaintive tone: "Oh, do tell me that Dr. Collyer has arrived! Do tell me that they have not contrived to intercept him, and that you have the package safe?"

"Madame," I replied—for her age and general appearance, as well as the fact that she was out alone at such an hour, clearly suggested to a man who had so long been party to Dupin's skill in ratiocination that she must be married, or a widow—"I have not the slightest idea what you are talking about, nor, for that matter, who you are."

Her response was to look behind her anxiously, as if she feared that she might have been followed to my doorstep—although the night was as black as ink, and could have hidden a dozen pursuers of any sort without offering the slightest clue as to their presence—and then to step forward, with a most unfeminine boldness, and force me to stand aside as she surged into my hallway uninvited.

"Please close the door," she said. "I shall be glad to explain who I am, and what mission brought me here, but I need to be safe from prying eyes. A man's life might be at stake—and more lives than one, if we have read the meaning of Chapelain's story rightly."

For a moment, I was heartily glad that Dupin was waiting in my sitting-room. Little as I cared about the good opinion of my

neighbors, I would not have wanted to be identified by anyone in the vicinity as the kind of man who routinely entertained dubious women in his house at the dead of night. To be sure, my unexpected visitor's costume encouraged the belief that she was respectable, but even whores can seem chaste when they need to mount a masquerade.

I showed my guest into the sitting-room, where Dupin was waiting, still sprawled in his armchair. His stockings were slightly singed, even though the fire was not blazing quite as brightly as we might have desired. He sprang to his feet, however, as soon as he caught our visitor—a convulsive return to nervous tension that might have saved the empty crystal glass in his hand from dropping from his nerveless fingers and shattering on the hearth. I reflected that it was most unlike him to be taken by surprise in that fashion. His ears were keen, and I would have expected him to make every effort to overhear what was said on the doorstep, given that he must have suspected, as I had, that the ringing doorbell signaled an appeal for help addressed to him. Evidently, he was uncommonly somnolent.

Whether it saved his wine-glass or not, Dupin's alacrity to demonstrate his politeness to our unexpected guest misfired. The suddenness of his action threw my visitor into a virtual panic. She clearly did not recognize Dupin, and evidently feared that any stranger might be an enemy. She spun around, and on finding my slightly corpulent frame blocking the doorway, appeared to think that she might have walked into a trap. She opened her mouth as if to scream, but controlled herself once again, and no sound came out.

"Calm yourself, Madame," I said, perhaps a little less compassionately than the situation warranted. "No one here means you any harm. This is the Chevalier Auguste Dupin, of whom you might have heard—the cleverest and most virtuous man in Paris, some would say. I regret, my friend, that I cannot complete the introduction, for the lady has not yet confided her name."

"Monsieur Dupin!" she exclaimed, as if suddenly overcome

by an enormous wave of relief. "I have heard your name, spoken in a highly complimentary context! Honoré has mentioned you, although he only knows you by reputation—by courtesy of Monsieur Vidocq, I believe. Honoré would like to meet you, I think...if that is any longer possible."

Dupin bowed. "I should be delighted to meet Monsieur Balzac, should a convenient opportunity present itself," he replied, with the utmost courtesy. I did not believe him at first, for he normally manifested an extreme reluctance to meet anyone, and took care to ensure that "convenient opportunities" of the kind he had cited never arose—but when the significance of the name sank in, I realized that this might be one instance in which he would gladly make an exception. Although his admiration for Monsieur Vidocq was carefully qualified and a trifle perverse, he had always been a sincere admirer of the supposed detective's most significant literary avatar, Jacques Collin, alias Vautrin—a character featured in several of the episodes of Monsieur Balzac's *Comédie humaine*—and he was a wholehearted devotee of the reclusive author's work.

"Do you know who I am, then?" my visitor asked, staring at Dupin with frank curiosity. "Have we met?"

"I have seen you in Père France's shop, Madame Hanska, and watched you inspecting the stock of the *bouquinistes* along the left bank of the Seine," Dupin admitted. "You were, inevitably, pointed out to me as a person of interest, but no one would have performed a reciprocal service for you, and you probably did not notice my drab presence. At any rate, we have not been formally introduced."

"Perhaps you could complete the introductions, Dupin," I suggested, "since you clearly have the advantage of me."

"Madame Ewelina Hanska," Dupin said, obligingly completing the name he had already mentioned—but he added no further information that might have enlightened me as to the lady's status, or the possible reason for her visit. He obviously assumed that I would recognize the name as that of Honoré de Balzac's mistress—although I might not have made the connec-

tion had the author's name not been mentioned already, as I am not a man to pay overmuch attention to gossip. Instead, Dupin addressed himself to the lady and said: "Are you looking for me, by any chance?"

"Why, no," she said. "It is your host that I came to see. I believe—or, at least, I hope—that he has a package recently arrived from New York, delivered privately, in order that he might take responsibility for its safe delivery into the hands of one of my fellow countrywomen."

Both my guests turned to look at me, expectantly, but all I could do was to strive as hard as I could not to look excessively foolish. "I am, alas, none the wiser," I said. "I have not received any package—and no dispatch at all from the American continent for three weeks, when I last heard word from my correspondent in New York."

"Oh dear God!" was Madame Hanska's response, as she put her hand to her brow as if in preparation to faint. "They have intercepted him! The Harmonic Society has anticipated us! Poor Collyer—they will have no compunction…." She stopped suddenly, as if realizing that she might have said too much.

Then she did faint—but Dupin, showing the dexterity and athleticism of which few men knew him to be capable, caught her in his arms and laid her gently down in the armchair he had vacated. Having made sure that she was secure, he stood up again, scratching his neatly-bearded chin pensively.

"Shall I look for some smelling-salts?" I asked, still feeling less compassionate than I ought to have been, because I still felt that I had been treated in a distinctly summary fashion.

"No," said Dupin. "You'd probably be better employed rooting out the latest issue of the *Journal de Magnétisme*, and the relevant copy of whichever American periodical it was that printed your friend's account of a strange mesmeric experiment a few weeks ago." When he had finished speaking, he leaned forward to touch the unconscious woman's forehead, in an oddly delicate and knowing manner, as if he were trying to establish some kind of psychic connection by physical means.

I did not move to take up his suggestions; I had not purchased a copy of the *Journal de Magnétisme* since the first issue had appeared the previous year. Curiosity is one thing, credulity another. I knew that Dupin had long been interested in the mysteries of animal magnetism, especially since its practice had become fashionable at the Saltpêtrière as a potential means of rendering patients insensitive to pain during surgical operations, but I had not thought him to be a firm believer in the more exotic virtues of magnetic sleep. Indeed, I had once heard him refer to the late Marquis de Puységur as a "charlatan", and so far as I knew, he did not have a high opinion of the would-be mages of the Philosophical Harmonic Society of Paris. As for my correspondent's account of the case of Ernest Valdemar, I considered it to be a horror story in his usual vein, which had cleverly distorted an actual incident in order to contrive a literary effect, after his customary method.

"Will she recover?" I asked Dupin, a trifle anxiously. One of the few things likely to be more prejudicial to a man's reputation in Paris than having a female visitor die in his house on the wrong side of midnight is to have the mistress of a famous writer die in his house on the wrong side of midnight, especially if her inamorata is busy penning anther masterpiece.

"Of course," Dupin replied, picking up Madame Hanska's wrist in order to measure her pulse. "The poor woman has apparently over-exerted herself in her hurry to get here, and she seems to have been direly disappointed by the news that the mysterious Mr. Collyer had not arrived with his equally-mysterious package. When her heart-rate has slowed down, it will cease to flutter, and normal blood-flow to the brain will be restored. Did she say anything to you at the door which might enable us to glean more information regarding her purpose in coming here?"

I had to rack my brain, which seemed a trifle fuddled, but I fished up the relevant nugget of information soon enough. "She mentioned the name Chapelain," I said.

"Ah!" he said, as if that explained everything.

"Who's Chapelain?" I asked.

"Pierre Chapelain, I presume," Dupin replied. "Doubtless one of the many physicians that Monsieur Balzac has consulted—his health is not good, I believe, and he worries about it intensely. I have watched Monsieur Chapelain at work more than once, in collaboration with the surgeon Jules Cloquet, and we have been introduced. I missed their more successful experiments, alas. The last operation I attended, a few months ago, was definitely not a success, and the patient died."

"Is Chapelain a member of the Harmonic Society?"

"I doubt it—but how would I know, since its membership list, and almost everything else about the society nowadays, is kept so rigorously secret? Its members did not react well to the criticisms leveled against it in the 1790s, and the new interest in mesmeric anesthesia generated by performances in the operating theater—especially Dupotet's recent endeavors—has not served to bring it out of its shell. If anything, it has had the opposite effect. Its inner circle insists on maintaining an esotericism that is as unwarranted as it is undesirable. If Bertrand had lived a decade longer, things might have worked our differently, but the poor fellow died at forty-two, whereas that clown Puységur lived to be a hundred. There's no justice in longevity, alas."

I had no idea how old Dupin was, although I had some reason to think his appearance deceptive. When we first met I had taken him for a young man, but had soon learned to doubt that judgment. He did not look a day over forty, but sometimes spoke as if he had witnessed the '89 revolution and had been on nodding terms with Napoléon Bonaparte before he became Emperor. That might have been mere affectation, in the Byronic mode that was enjoying a resurgence of fashionability, but the fact that he evaded all direct questions on the subject seemed to me to be more than a mere attempt to cultivate an image.

"You're referring to Alexandre Bertrand, the spiritualist," I said, ever-eager not to be taken for a clod.[1]

---

1. For the benefit of any American readers who might come across this memoir, if it should ever chance to be printed, I ought perhaps to explain that in 1846, the

"The very same," he confirmed.

"But wasn't Puységur a spiritualist also?" I asked, hesitantly. "Weren't he and Bertrand birds of a feather, united against the materialism of the physiologists when it came to explaining the supposed phenomena of magnetism?"

"By virtue of its positivist policy of blunt denial," Dupin informed me, loftily, "there is only one kind of materialism, and hence only one brand of physiological mesmerism. There are, however, several distinct schools of spiritualist mesmerism, which differ sharply in their interpretations of somniloquism."

"Is that the same as somnambulism?" I asked.

"Only in the sense that the oral phenomenon that is correctly called somniloquism is often mistakenly called somnambulism, which obviously ought to refer to sleep-*walking*—but hush now; our enigmatic visitor is coming round."

Madame Hanska was indeed showing signs of life. I bent down to stir up the fire, thinking that warmth might have as much reviving effect as smelling-salts, and do her a great deal more good.

---

word "spiritualism" did not have the meaning it subsequently acquired when it was appropriated as the name of a religion. The sensation launched by the exploits of the Fox sisters did not materialize until 1848; in the years preceding that date, the term was principally used in the context of a fervent debate between rival schools of mesmerists—"spiritualists" and "physiologists"—who disagreed as to the kind of explanation that required to be sought for the phenomena of "animal magnetism".

CHAPTER TWO

Madame Hanska's Story

"Oh dear!" said Ewelina Hanska, when she finally realized where she was and what had happened. "I'm so very sorry, gentlemen. You must think me a poor fool—like one of your delicate little Parisian coquettes rather than the mature and sturdy Polish patriot that I am—or try to be."

Dupin had already leaned over to the mantelpiece. The mulled wine had all been drunk, but we had not made any inroads into the decanter of brandy. He poured her a generous glass, which she accepted gratefully. He and I exchanged a glance as the lady bowed her head to take a sip, and I could see that he seemed unusually perplexed. He stroked his beard again, and seemed to be making a definite effort to collect himself. I was as puzzled as he was by the fact that he had not reverted to full alertness with his usual alacrity—but his effort seemed to be successful, and when he spoke again, his voice was resolute and his attention focused.

"Now, Madame" he said, as the lady took a second generous sip of eau-de-vie, "perhaps you would care to explain what it is that your Monsieur Collyer was supposed to be bringing here. If it really has gone astray, my friend and I will be happy to do everything we can to assist in its recovery. If necessary, I have the ear of the Prefect of Police."

"Oh! No police, I beg you. My friend would not like that at all!" Her tone was anxious.

"The friend in question being Mademoiselle Valdemar, I

presume?"

There was a further flicker of anxiety in Madame Hanska's eyes, but she made an effort to remove all indication of it from her voice. "How could you possibly know that, Monsieur Dupin?" she asked.

"Don't be alarmed—it was mere logical deduction, in the great tradition of Voltaire's Zadig. You have already mentioned the Harmonic Society and Dr. Chapelain, which informs me that mesmerism lies at the heart of the matter in question, and you mentioned that your friend was a fellow countrywoman. Our host has, of course, shown me his American correspondent's account of the experiment carried out in New York on the Polish scholar Ernest Valdemar, rumor of which reached Paris some while ago, its interest enhanced by the residence in the city of Monsieur Valdemar's lovely daughter. The presumption that the mesmerist who entranced Valdemar, and who told the story to Mr. Poe, must have asked Poe's advice as to whether he knew anyone trustworthy in Paris, who might assist in ensuring that Valdemar's effects could be delivered to his heiress discreetly and intact, seemed to be a mere matter of mental arithmetic. Am I correct?"

"More correct than you know, Monsieur Dupin. I would not have thought to refer to the consignment as Monsieur Valdemar's *effects*—but that, hopefully, is what they might turn out to be."

"And who is this Monsieur Collyer?" Dupin asked, evidently enthusiastic to get down to brass tacks now that he made a rough sketch of the problem's shape and dimensions.

"*Doctor* Collyer is an English mesmerist—a friend and colleague of the practitioner who told Mr. Poe the story of the Valdemar experiment, although not one of the two who collaborated with Poe's informant in the experiment itself. Dr. Collyer returned to England in January. Whether he brought...the effects...with him, or whether they were subsequently brought to him in London, I don't know. At any rate, he graciously offered to bring them with him to Paris when next he visited the Saltpêtrière, as he does on a regular basis, to confer with

Monsieur Dupotet, and to confide them to a trustworthy agent capable of locating Jana Valdemar, who would deliver the consignment to her in the strictest confidence." She turned to look at me, with a gaze that now seemed keen and full of intelligence. "Mr. Poe had assured Dr. Collyer that you were exactly the man for the job."

My American correspondent was, I knew full well, a close ally as well as a hapless victim of what he called "the imp of the perverse". I suspected that in recommending my services, he might really have been recommending Dupin's, and very wisely too, given that Dupin had an unparalleled talent for finding things—especially things that might be better left hidden—and sorting out difficult matters in the strictest confidence.

I blushed slightly as the wry codicil to that thought drifted into my mind, rather inappropriately—I had no reason, as yet, to think that Mademoiselle Valdemar might belong to the category of things best left hidden, and it seemed impolite even to entertain the accidental suggestion.

"And why do you and Mademoiselle Valdemar think that the Harmonic Society might be interested in intercepting Dr. Collyer?" Dupin persisted.

"Because they might well think, if they have received the same intelligence of the experiment that was communicated to Dr. Chapelain, that the effects are precious, in the context of their beliefs and ambitions."

"I presume that we are not talking merely in terms of monetary value?"

"The President of the Harmonic Society might not be thinking in such terms at all," Madame Hanska said, a trifle hesitantly, "any more than I am—but there are others who probably would, if they got wind of the consignment's nature. It is possible that Dr. Collyer might have been followed from London—or from New York, if that is where he first acquired the parcel—as well as highly probable that there is more than one person in Paris who would be glad to rifle through his luggage."

"I see," said Dupin. He paused for thought then, in an osten-

tatious manner that I recognized very well indeed.

"Is there a Harmonic Society in New York too?" I asked, curiously, of no one in particular. "There's more than one in Paris, I know, and at least one in London."

It was Ewelina Hanska who took it upon herself to answer. "One of the collaborators in the Valdemar experiment was Andrew Jackson Davis," she reported, "who embraces what he calls the Harmonial Philosophy—but I have no particular reason to believe that he has any sinister agenda."

I had been associated with Dupin long enough to take the immediate inference from that remark that Madame Hanska *did* have reason to believe that the Philosophical Harmonic Society of Paris, or some of its members, might have a sinister agenda of some kind. I nodded—sagely, I hoped.

"John Elliotson of *The Zoist*, England's leading spiritualist, was associated with the London Harmonic Society before his fall from grace," Madame Hanska added, "but I doubt that he is a villain, in spite of his discredit. Jana has mentioned him in complimentary terms—and she knows his mentor quite well, I think."

I did not like to ask who Elliotson's mentor might be, lest I seem ignorant of matters with which she assumed me to be familiar—but Dupin was ready to step into the breach again and provide a tacit answer to the question. "Yes," he said, as if the true dimensions of the affair were now becoming obvious to him. "We must go to see Dupotet, of course. If he cannot enlighten us as to Collyer's whereabouts…you're quite sure that Mademoiselle Valdemar wants the police kept out of it?"

"Absolutely certain," Madame Hanska replied, firmly.

"In that case, I shall make my own investigation of Dr. Collyer's itinerary, and then report back to Mademoiselle Valdemar herself, if I may."

Our visitor's face clouded slightly at that, and she finished her brandy in a single gulp that was not entirely ladylike. "Mademoiselle Valdemar would rather her whereabouts remained unknown, for the time being," she said. "We would

prefer it if you could use me as an intermediary in communicating with her."

"Of course," said Dupin, immediately. "It shall be as you wish—and I give you my word that, if Monsieur Valdemar's effects *have* gone astray, we shall do everything within our power to return them to their rightful owner."

Madame Hanska stood up. "Have you a piece of paper and a pen?" she asked me.

"Only a goose-quill, I fear," I said. "Old habits die hard, and I have never quite accustomed myself to steel nibs."

"Monsieur Balzac swears by them," she observed, as she accepted the quill and a leaf of paper. She scribbled an address and handed it back to me, saying: "You can contact me there— the concierge will take a message if I am not at home. She's very reliable, in spite of her unprepossessing appearance."

"Whoever heard of a concierge whose appearance was not unprepossessing?" Dupin asked, lightly. He did not, I observed, make the corollary observation that no one ever heard of one who was reliable either. "You say that you have received intelligence of the Valdemar experiment, which presumably goes further than Mr. Poe's account. Am I right in thinking that the intelligence in question came from Dr. Chapelain?"

"Yes, indeed. He told us that...."

Dupin held up his hand. "I shall go to see Chapelain too," he said. "I know him slightly, and he will tell me the story himself. That way, I can interrogate him as to his own source, and press him on the finer details of the story. We really should not keep you here any longer, Madame Hanska, given the lateness of the hour."

"I'm well used to keeping strange hours," she assured us. "Honoré...."

Again, Dupin cut her off. She seemed slightly surprised by his manner—as I was myself. I could only conclude that he felt so tired that he wanted to make a fresh start on the problem in the morning, and felt that he could not give it the concentrated attention it deserved until then.

We showed Madame Hanska to the door, and I offered to find her a cab. She refused, assuring me that she would be perfectly safe in spite of the hour, the cold and the dark. I would have accepted her assurance—she was, after all, not a little Parisian coquette but a mature and sturdy Pole—but Dupin would not hear of it. He demanded that she wait on the doorstep until he had collected his coat, hat and cane.

I drifted within him toward the coat-rack. "What on Earth do you make of all this?" I whispered.

"I don't know enough, as yet, to make anything of it," he replied, "and my mind seems to be in no fit condition to work on it—but I intend to repair that ignorance and unreadiness as soon as possible. May I collect you at eight sharp, so that we can go to see Dupotet and Chapelain?"

"Of course, if you so wish," I said, earnestly. "Should I take the risk of absenting myself from the house, though, while there is still a possibility that this mysterious parcel might arrive?"

"Would you rather stay here, then, while I investigate?" he asked. He knew that I liked to watch him at work—and was probably aware, too, that his own second-hand accounts of his investigations often left something to be desired.

I assured him that, if he thought it best for me to accompany him, I would certainly do so. I could not, however, resist the temptation to stop him as he made as if to rejoin Madame Hanska in order to see her safely to the cab-rank on the Boulevard. "Why didn't you interrogate Madame Hanska more closely as to exactly what is in the mysterious package that Dr. Collyer was supposed to be bringing here?" I asked. "Do you know more than you're letting on?"

"No," Dupin admitted, "but she seems reluctant to spell it out, and there must be a reason for her embarrassment; delicate diplomacy might be in order in that respect. At any rate, she has said exactly what she intended to say on that matter, and I would not have obtained more from her by interrogation."

"Do you think her urgency and fainting fit were mere matters of performance, then?" I asked, mildly astonished—but still

speaking in a conscientious whisper.

"Performance, certainly, in a manner of speaking—mere, no. She really does feel that the matter is urgent and problematic, perhaps on behalf of Monsieur Balzac as well as her friend Mademoiselle Valdemar, but she came here with a role to play, and played it. She was very anxious to know whether Collyer had arrived, but she was determined to move you to action if he had not, and was fully prepared to make whatever appeal to your good nature might be necessary."

"But if she isn't entirely sure what the package contains…." I began, still trying to formulate the thought as I began to voice it.

Dupin cut me off in a peremptory manner. "The point is evidently not so much what the package actually contains, as what it intended recipient and potential interceptors believe that its *effects* might be. The first thing we need to discover is what Saint-Germain believes it to be, and why he seems it sufficiently valuable to be worthy committing a crime."

"Saint-Germain?" I queried, assuming that he meant the suburb to the west of my residence, and that he was using the term—as almost everyone else in Paris did—to refer to what Bostonians call "high society".

"An old friend," he said, softly. "Or, to be strictly accurate, an old adversary."

"A criminal or a book-collector?" I joked, all too well aware of the two classes of men he regarded as his natural adversaries.

"Both," he replied, succinctly. "But I must not keep Madame Hanska waiting in the freezing cold any longer—until eight o'clock, then. *Au revoir.*" And he bolted through the door, exhibiting a combination of urgency and weariness that was by no means typical of him, even when there was mischief afoot.

I closed the door behind him and immediately put my hands to my head. It was not aching, in the way it sometimes did when I came down with a migraine, but it felt distinctly odd, as if my brain no longer belonged entirely to me. I returned to the sitting-room, intending to take a restorative glass of brandy myself, but I found, once the mental stimulus of company and conversation

was removed, that I was extraordinarily tired. I felt in dire need of sleep, and hurried my preparations for bed—although, as I have mentioned, I am not the sort of person who is generally overtaken by tiredness during the hours of darkness.

CHAPTER THREE
A Sequence of Nightmares

I expected to fall asleep as soon as my head hit the pillow, and I suppose that I must have done, but I eventually found myself disturbed and pinned down by a strange nightmare, in which I was pursued by a strange creature with blazing eyes, which sometimes glided and sometimes crept, but never relieved me of the furious impact of its stare. It was a monster, I knew, but it was also—in some strange fashion that was in perfect accordance with the logic of the dream—a beautiful woman.

The pursuit seemed to go on for an eternity, although I knew enough about dreams to be well aware, once I become conscious of the fact that I was dreaming, that it had probably lasted no more than a few seconds of real time, and that its apparent extension in the past might even have been a delusion. At any rate, it ended—or, at least, seemed to end—when I was finally captured, at which point, the loathsome but radiant individual said, quite distinctly and in a remarkably seductive tone of voice: "Kiss me, my mortal lover!"

Such is the logic of dreams that I should have woken up at this point, and I thought that I did, with my heart pounding, struggling to open my eyes. After another interval of time that probably seemed far longer than it was, I did contrive to lift my eyelids, at least fractionally, but my sight was inevitably confused by the flame of the night-light I maintained on my beside table. I thought, however, that I caught a glimpse of two staring eyes before I heard my bedroom door close with a

sinister click.

It was at that point that I realized that I must still be dreaming, and that I had merely carried forward the image, or at least the idea, of the Dweller of the Threshold from one segment of the nightmare to another. Oddly enough, the realization that the nightmare had not ended did not serve to renew my anxiety, but rather to soothe it, and unthinkingly putting a name to the monster—which identified it as a creature of fiction—was a further relief. I slipped back once again into sleep of a more peaceful sort.

Given that I had gone to sleep again once the two phases of the nightmare had run their course, and had slept more peacefully, I was slightly surprised to wake up again, after an interval that might have been an hour of real time, to find that I could still remember the bad dream quite distinctly, and that I was possessed of a certain pride in the knowledge that I already had a perfectly sane explanation of the dream's contents.

Only a few days before, I had finished reading Edward Bulwer-Lytton's sensational romance *Zanoni*, which had become one of the literary phenomena of the decade, and my dream had been a straightforward re-enactment of one of its most famous scenes, in which the novice Glyndon unwisely disobeys the prohibition placed jupon him by his mentor Mejnour, and attempts to press forward too rapidly with his initiation into the mysteries of Rosicrucian magic. His rash action exposes him to the Dweller of the Threshold, the seemingly-female creature I had perceived in my dream, who pursues him in exactly the same way, and finally confronts him with the same dire demand—in response to which he faints.

I made a mental note to ask my American correspondent, the next time I wrote to him, whether he had read the novel—which seemed to me to be very much his sort of thing—but then I had to put the matter out of my mind in order to concentrate on the real world. I had to dress in a hurry, washing in cold water because I did not have time to boil a kettle. I was ready in time for Dupin to pick me up at eight, though, and even had

a minute or two to spare—an interval that I spent standing in the stairway, with my fur-lined coat and gloves on. I had an odd sensation that I was not alone, and that staring eyes might be fixed upon me, but when I turned around and saw nothing, I realized that it must be a residuum of my nightmare, which had not yet let go of me entirely, even though I was now fully awake.

"Get thee behind me, amorous demon!" I said, aloud, trying to laugh. I might have felt my failure more keenly had Dupin not arrived just then, ready to bear me away into a daylit adventure—if the leaden grey of the morning sky really deserved the appellation "daylight".

"Did you sleep well?" I asked Dupin, as our fiacre rattled along the quai marking the edge of the Faubourg Saint-Victor. The question seemed warranted, given his sour expression and slightly sullen silence

"I did not," he said, a trifle resentfully—although I could not see that I was in any way responsible for his bad mood. A partial explanation was supplied when he added: "I don't know what new spice it was that you added to the mix of that mulled wine, but I think you ought to avoid it in future."

I decided to ignore the blatant unfairness of the remark. "I had a nightmare myself," I told him, instead, "in which I re-enacted a scene from *Zanoni*. Not entirely apt, given that we had spent the night discussing matters arising from 'The Facts in the Case of M. Valdemar'—but the mind routinely plays such deceptive tricks, does it not? Do you suppose that Bulwer has read Poe, and Poe Bulwer?"

Dupin looked at me rather strangely, almost with suspicion. "I presume so," he replied, eventually, a trifle warily, "since everyone in the world seems to have read *Zanoni*—but I doubt that there has been any direct influence between the two. With reference to the two works you have just cited, the two authors have merely drawn the water of inspiration from the same well. Such ideas are very much in the air at present—as you are certainly aware."

I was, indeed. They were rather more "in the air" in my

house than most Parisian interiors; Dupin and I had discussed many books in the course of our acquaintance that dealt with such notions, often in peculiar ways. Some of our adventures had brought us into contact with similar ideas made manifest, although I was never entirely clear in my own mind as to whether their ambiguous aspects might only *seem* supernatural, precisely because of the turn of mind that we had cultivated in our reading, with assistance from the likes of Poe and Bulwer. Before I could launch into a discussion of that potentially-interesting issue, however, I needed a clearer head, and for the moment I was glad simply to feel the chill wind of our passage through a crack in the fiacre's ill-fitting *portière*. I felt that I needed a blast of winter to clear the lingering discomfort from my brain.

I did not speak again until the cab turned right at the corner of the Jardin des Plantes, and then it was only to remark on the seeming stillness of the Seine, whose current seemed hardly visible.

The fiacre drew up at the main gate of the Saltpêtrière shortly thereafter, and Dupin rushed off. By the time I had paid the coachman he was twenty meters ahead, and I did not catch up with him until we were at the very door of the operating theater—where a different kind of nightmare was just about to begin.

That was the first time I clapped eyes on Jules-Denis Dupotet, who had only recently begun to style himself the "Baron du Potet", and had not yet added the further cognomen "de Sennevoy". I knew his reputation, though; he was the best-known experimenter in animal magnetism in France now that Puységur was dead. Their careers had only overlapped slightly, Puységur having been extremely old when he had died in 1825, and Dupotet having been relatively young—only in his twenties—when he had begun his famous series of experiments in 1821.[2]

---

2. Again, because times have changed, it may be necessary to add a comment here about the stage that Dupotet's career had reached in February of 1846. Although

My first impression on actually seeing Dupotet in the flesh was that he was not as tall as I had expected—but he did cut an imposing figure, standing in the center of that strange arena. He was not working in association with Cloquet today, but with a dentist named Salvagnac, who was about to undertake the extraction of two inconvenient molars from the jaw of a minor Academician. We had arrived just in time to see Dupotet induce the magnetic sleep that was supposed to ensure that the Academician felt no pain during the operation, so we were able to see him in action, making his mysterious passes and murmuring suggestions that were supposed to be subtle and private.

What struck me most of all about the entire procedure, I must admit, was the extraordinarily mixed reaction of the audience. The whole purpose of an operating theater, of course, is to allow students to watch their masters at work, but the recent practice of allowing access to the theater by scholars of other kinds had swelled the usual numbers considerably, especially with respect to operations involving mesmeric anesthesis. I knew, of course, that such practises had become the focus of considerable controversy of late, but I had not realized how fierce that controversy had become until I watched Dupotet at work—or

he is now best known as the author of the sensational *Magie dévoilée*, he did not publish that book until 1852; all his publications prior to 1846 had detailed his own experiments in mesmerism, with particular reference to the medical uses of so-called magnetic sleep. These reports emphasized the soberly empirical over the theoretically speculative, and their substance encouraged the supposition that the author was a Comtean physiologist who refused to make the assumption that the phenomena of animal magnetism were in any way supernatural. *Magie dévoilée*, of course, revealed him to be the very opposite: a spiritualist of the most ambitious sort, committed to the belief that all phenomena previously considered to be magical were phenomena of a mesmeric kind, and that the study of animal magnetism would ultimately lead to a complete human mastery of magic. No one knows when he changed the direction of his thinking—if, indeed, he changed it at all—but the relevant point to note with respect to the present narrative is that when Dupin and I went to see him, on the morning after Madame Hanska's unexpected visit, we did so in the expectation, however vague, that he was unlikely to have imagined that there was anything supernatural about the phenomena observed in the case of Ernest Valdemar, or any similar occurrence.

trying to work—that morning.

I had not had the privilege of being present at any of the early performances of Victor Hugo's *Hernani*, which had taken place some years before my settlement in Paris, but I imagine that they must have been not unlike what I witnessed that day at the Saltpêtrière, with rival claques proudly taking up their positions like detachments of soldiers before a battle, and then allowing their enthusiasm to overflow in an uneasily muted manner, in the full knowledge that there were at least some people in the audience who merely wanted to see and hear the play with a minimum of distraction. Dupotet had to appeal for silence before he began his procedure, and had to interrupt himself more than once to make further, increasingly desperate, appeals, as the enemies of mesmerism let their feelings leak out in hostile whispers and suppressed catcalls, while the attempts made by the defenders of the new science to silence them only added to the inconvenient rumor.

I have to admit that the experiment was not a success—that the Academician, in spite of his best efforts to co-operate with the anesthetist, eventually began to howl in agony as the pincers got to work—but I really have no idea whether the failure was due to inherent flaws in Dupotet's technique or to the fact that the circumstances were so blatantly unconducive to success. The enemies of the supposed new science were, of course, in no doubt that they had simply witnessed yet another failure of a false system, and yet another proof of mesmeric charlatanry, but his supporters seemed equally convinced that Dupotet had been deliberately sabotaged, and would undoubtedly have succeeded in his attempt to nullify the Academician's pain had he not been prevented from doing so by the rival claque's noisy interference. It was, however, the supporters rather than the detractors who were primarily responsible for the crescendo effect that eventually allowed the noise from the audience to increase to the point at which it almost rivalled the unfortunate patient's screams.

When the operation was over, Dupotet lingered briefly in the center of the room while Salvagnac fled, bearing away the

unfortunate patient and his rotten molars, delicately balanced on a silver-plated salver. The mesmerist did not say anything to the audience, but he did fix the loudest of his accusers with a basilisk stare of the sort that gave rise to the expression "If looks could kill…." Even a mesmerist of his stature, however, evidently lacked that kind of power, at least at the relevant distance—but once again, I had a momentary reminder of my nightmare, and had to suppress a shudder. Then the great man strode away, as majestically as a lion, undefeated in site of his apparent failure.

Dupin and I were obliged to queue outside an anteroom of the theater once the molars had been bloodily removed, but we were swiftly moved to the head of the queue once the door was opened—thus attracting the envy of several other interested parties who had sent in their cards along with ours, but to whom the privilege of an interview was peremptorily refused.

The anteroom was more like a store-room or a trophy-room than a reception-room, in spite of its armchairs and occasional tables. Its walls were entirely lined with shelves, and the shelves were crowded with bottles and jars, all of them containing diseased organs extracted by surgeons over the course of at least two decades. The labels in the jars identified each organ and the disease that had afflicted it, but gave no clue as to the method of anesthesia used—if any—to facilitate their excision. The tooth-marks deeply engraved in an assortment of thick leather straps hanging on hooks behind the door, however, clearly testified to the dire need that contemporary surgeons had for more efficient means of pain-control than dosing their patients with hard liquor or laudanum.

The sight of the pickled organs and the odor of the preservatives in which they were embalmed made me slightly nauseous, but at least there were no staring eyes among them, let alone insistent lips.

"Welcome to my battleground, Monsieur Dupin," said Dupotet, when the orderly who had ushered us in had given us wooden stools to sit on. "I've heard of you, of course—and

I believe that I've seen you in the theater before. I must apologize for the near-riot, but it seems that the lines have now been clearly drawn and the troops formed up, and that any further possibility of a fair and honest test of the efficacy of magnetic sleep as a means of anesthesia must be ruled out. The establishment feels that its cherished ideas and time-worn customs are under threat, and must react—even if its actions obliterate progress and condemn those in dire need of surgery to continue to suffer traumatic shock, with all its terrors and dangers. It's not merely stupid but wicked."

"You have my sympathies, Baron," said Dupin, smoothly. "In such circumstances as those we have just witnessed, one can hardly blame the Philosophical Harmonic Society for its refusal to let its own experiments be witnessed by outsiders, and its insistence on maintaining a veil of secrecy over its methods and designs."

I observed that Dupotet's eyes narrowed slightly at mention of the Harmonic Society, and he was conspicuous in his avoidance of any explicit response to the conversational gambit. "How can I help you, Monsieur Dupin?" he said. "I'm sorry to be so unceremonious, but I'm a busy man. I hope that you are not here on behalf of the Prefecture?"

"Oh no," Dupin was quick to reassure him. "I am merely making enquiries on behalf of a friend about the whereabouts of Dr. Robert Collyer, whose arrival in Paris seems to be overdue. He was, I believe, intending to visit you?"

"I was expecting him yesterday morning," the mesmerist confirmed, "but I am not unduly worried by his lateness. It's February, after all, and channel crossings are very often delayed at his time of year. The diligences from Calais and Boulogne sometimes find that roads so difficult that they suffer delays of a day or more."

"I have been to the *Messageries générales* within the last two hours," Dupin said, mildly. "The director confirms that the main roads have been clear of snow for the last two days, and that no delays longer than two hours have been recorded. The

coachmen have reported that ferry crossings from Dover and Folkestone have not suffered any serious interruption by bad weather."

"Ah," said Dupotet. "In that case…." He trailed off, evidently to signify that he was at a loss.

"I have also visited the Morgue," Dupin added. He had evidently risen early and put in a good deal of effort before pausing to collect me. "There is no body on exhibition there whose clothing indicates that it might be that of an Englishman, or any belonging to a male of the relevant age." He paused before adding, in a deliberately sinister tone: "Which does not mean, of course, that Dr Collyer might not have met with misfortune before ever reaching the *barrière*."

CHAPTER FOUR

The Baron Becomes Anxious

Dupotet reacted to Dupin's speech with evident alarm. "You think Collyer might be dead?" he said, his astonishment seemingly unfeigned. "Why on Earth would you assume that? It's far more likely that his departure was delayed by urgent claims in London. He is a physician, after all—and shameful displays like the one you have just witnessed do not detract from the demands currently being made on magnetizers, I can assure you."

"I don't doubt it," said Dupin. "And I confess that I have not yet been able to ascertain whether, or when, Dr. Collyer actually left London—but my friend is anxious, on account of a consignment that he was supposed to be bringing with him." He turned to look at me, ostentatiously, although he was careful not to say explicitly that I was the friend to whom he was referring.

Dupotet glanced at my card again, to check my name—which was of course, quite unfamiliar to him. Helpfully, I put in: "I believe that the package originated in New York, although it might have been passed on to Dr. Collyer in London. The suggestion that he use me as a further intermediary was made by my American correspondent, Edgar Poe."

Dupotet had heard of Poe, just as he had heard of Dupin. I did not doubt, either, that he had read Poe's account of the Valdemar affair, and that his mental arithmetic, even it were not the equal of Dupin's, would be up to the task of putting two and two together without going far wrong.

"You mean that Collyer was bringing Valdemar's remains

to Paris?" the mesmerist said. "And not to me, but to *you?*" I did not like the almost-contemptuous manner in which he pronounced the word *you*.

"I am not sure what the exact contents of the package are," I said, stiffly, "but I have been reliably informed that it was supposed to be delivered to my address, in the first instance, in order that I might convey it to its ultimate destination."

"To me, you mean?" he said, jumping to entirely the wrong conclusion. "But why wouldn't Collyer bring the package directly to me? What is he afraid...?" He stopped abruptly—not, this time, merely for effect.

"As you pointed out only a moment ago," Dupin put in, still speaking very smoothly, "and as was clearly evident in the operating theater, there are people intent on disrupting your work. Perhaps the catcallers in your audience today—or, more likely, the paymasters who funded the claque—would be interested in knowing what Dr. Collyer's parcel contains...or even in preventing it from reaching its intended recipient?"

Dupotet had gone pale. He evidently believed—as Dupin had allowed him to do, without actually telling him an outright lie—that Collyer's consignment had been ultimately intended for him, and was wondering what its possible interception might signify. "No," he said, in a fashion that seemed quite involuntary. "He wouldn't...." Again, he stopped abruptly.

"Who wouldn't, Baron?" Dupin was swift to ask, in the same silky tone—but the ploy misfired. Dupotet had already collected himself, and had no intention of giving away any more.

"Thank you, gentlemen," the mesmerist was quick to say, now intent on ending the interview. "I'm in your debt. I had no idea that there might be any sinister implication in Robert's lateness, and it's very good of you to take the trouble to worry on his behalf. I shall make what enquiries I can."

"Will you approach Mademoiselle Valdemar, or shall I?" Dupin enquired, as quick as a flash.

Dupotet was caught off guard, and had already answered: "I will," before it even occurred to him to wonder whether he

should have reacted to the young woman's name at all. Swiftly, but uncertainly, he added: "Do you know Mademoiselle Valdemar, then, Monsieur Dupin?"

"Only by reputation," Dupin replied, airily. "She's said to be a very fine medium—Chapelain thinks so, I believe—but I've never seen her in…performance. Doubtless you've conducted your own experiments. Is it because the writer in New York was her father that he was chosen for the American experiment, do you think? Sensitivity is supposed to have a hereditary component, is it not? Or do you agree with Elliotson in believing that woman are far more sensitive than men, and that uneducated women are less likely to be blinded in their sensitivity by their own intelligence?"

Dupotet was confused by the sheer complexity of this series of prompts—as Dupin had presumably intended—but he replied, as if reflexively: "Elliotson is wrong, and his predilection for dull-witted Irish maidens has not served his cause, alas. Mademoiselle Valdemar is proof enough that intelligence is no inhibitor of sensitivity."

"Quite the reverse, in fact," Dupin supplied. "I agree with you wholeheartedly, Baron. Will you be publishing the record of your experiments with Mademoiselle Valdemar in the near future? I would be very interested to read them."

Dupotet's guard was up again, alas. "Perhaps," he said, with a deliberate vagueness that suggested negativity. "I really am sorry, gentlemen, but I cannot entertain you any longer. As I said, the demands on my time…." This time, the dangling sentence was entirely calculated.

"Of course, Baron, of course," Dupin was quick to say. "We're terribly sorry to have disturbed you, and I hope with all my heart that my anxieties are misplaced, and the Dr. Collyer will materialize very soon, able and eager to deliver his consignment."

Dupin was already ushering me out of the anteroom. I was grateful for that; I must confess that the odor of formaldehyde was beginning to make my head swim in a most unpleasant

manner. I deduced from his urgency to be gone that, even if my friend had not discovered everything he wanted to know, he had discovered everything he thought recoverable from Dupotet, at least for the moment. I allowed myself to be propelled along the corridors of the hospital, and was glad when we reached the open air again.

"What a horrid place!" I exclaimed. "I'm a passionate devotee of the theater, as you know—but that one was reminiscent of the Roman amphitheater at its worst. I had no idea that medical education in the heart of Paris had been reduced to the status of a sadistic circus!"

"The divine Marquis might well have found it amusing," Dupin mused, distractedly. "There is, alas, a determined war being waged over the claims of mesmerists, whose combatants have little interest in the objective accumulation of evidence. The battle of the anesthetics cannot last, of course—but I fear that the likely manner of its settlement might obliterate any chance that remains of a rational arbitration of the question of the potential utility of magnetic sleep."

"What are you talking about?" I asked, in frank bewilderment.

"Ether," he said, succinctly, as he hailed a cab and leapt in. "But that's not important, for now. We must get on." Once I had climbed up beside him he continued: "I'm sorely tempted to call on Monsieur Balzac, who might prove far more loquacious than his mistress or the good doctor, if he is not sick in bed—but rumor has it that, when he is well, he often works or ten or twelve hours at a stretch, beginning at midnight, and that he hates to be disturbed. The only safe time to call on him when he is not confined to his bed is in the late afternoon, before he goes to sleep at six o'clock. Ergo, we shall now go in search of Pierre Chapelain—and if he is not at home, we shall go to the Prefecture. We must be back at your house by noon, though."

"You don't intend to take any notice of Madame Hanska's insistence that the police be left out of it, then?" I said, as the cab thundered along in the direction of the *place* where the

Bastille once stood.

"I would not dream of breaking a promise made to a lady," Dupin replied, "even though the undertaking in question was more tacit than explicit. The Prefecture's clerks are however, extraordinarily scrupulous, if a little belated, in recording the comings and goings of foreign nationals, especially the English—a hangover from the war years. I merely want to consult their registers with regard to Dr. Collyer's previous visits, to ascertain where he normally stays, and the acquaintances he has previously kept. If he's in hiding, we might be able to obtain a clue as to his whereabouts."

"You think he might be in hiding?"

"I have no idea—all possibilities are open, at present, and I'm reluctant to leave any unexplored."

"But you are taking this business very seriously? Otherwise, you wouldn't have gone to the Morgue."

"It's an intriguing puzzle," he replied. "You know how I love puzzles."

I did. "And how many pieces of the jigsaw did Dupotet provide, wittingly or unwittingly?" I asked, curiously.

"Precious few, I fear," Dupin admitted. "I suspect that we told him at least as much as he told us. He really had not read anything untoward into Collyer's lateness, and evidently had no idea that Collyer was carrying what he assumed to be Valdemar's *remains*...a word as ambiguously suggestive, in its way, as *effects*. He seemed to conclude that someone might be playing him false, though, and to resent the fact."

"Chapelain?" I asked.

"Perhaps." That was another *perhaps* that had a distinct ring of negativity about it.

"Saint-Germain, then?" I guessed. I knew his methods, and only had to apply them, as best I could.

He looked at me sharply. "Perhaps," he said, again—but in a different tone.

"Saint-Germain of the Harmonic Society, I presume," I continued, feeling quite pleased with myself. I glanced out of

the window as we turned left on to the Rue Saint-Antoine.

"The very same," he conceded.

"A mesmerist and a spiritualist, then," I concluded, like the master of deduction I aspired to be. "A secretive one—and an old adversary of yours. Is he a charlatan, like Puységur?"

"No," he answered, curling his lip slightly. "Puységur was an honest charlatan, who deluded himself before he deluded others. The self-styled Comte is not so naïve."

I had not made the connection before, but I could hardly help making it then. "The *Comte* de Saint-Germain?" I queried. "That's the name adopted by a supposed magician who caused a stir in the last century. Was he really immortal, then, as he is said to have claimed?"

"Perhaps," he said, yet again, in a very muted tone. "Far more probably, his present incarnation is an ambitious inheritor of the original masquerader's name and his impostures. I am not in a position either to confirm or deny that the man who wears the guise now is the same one who manifested himself in the days before the Revolution, although I feel fully entitled to doubt his claim—but if he is a brazen liar, as I suspect, he's no less dangerous for that. If Dupotet has become involved with him, it's a pity—and if Mademoiselle Valdemar is involved with him...."

I had had enough of dangling sentences, for the time being. "Well, what?" I demanded, brutally.

"Then she might be in danger," Dupin finished, obligingly. "And Madame Hanska too...not to mention the second greatest writer in France."

"Balzac, you mean?" I said. I did not have to ask to whom the great novelist came second; even Balzac, who was reputed not to be a modest man, would have had to admit that he had not yet outshone Victor Hugo.

Dupin did not reply, partly because it was unnecessary, and partly because we had reached our destination, in the streets on the western edge of the Faubourg Saint-Antoine. He had already leapt to the ground, and was hastening to consult the concierge

of the nearest building as to the whereabouts of Dr. Chapelain—
leaving me, as usual, to pay the coachman.

CHAPTER FIVE
The Elixir of Life

Pierre Chapelain's apartment was surprisingly modest, given that he was one of the most sought-after physicians in the capital, numbering several députés among his clients as well as notable literary men, and being no stranger to the other, more respectable, Saint-Germain. His fees were obviously less than usurious—which was something else, I gathered, that the physicians of the monopolist establishment had against such upstarts and *parvenus* as the various followers of Anton Mesmer and Samuel Hahnemann.

There were no collections of extracted teeth and organs on display in the doctor's study, although there was the usual assembly of anatomical diagrams that one expects to find in the working space of any trained physician, left over from his student days and maintained as *aides memoires* or badges of office. The bookshelves, as might be expected, were loaded with standard publications on mesmerism, with Simon Mialle's massive compendium of evidence—most of it, alas, anecdotal—taking pride of place. I was interested to note that, in addition to dozens of volumes in French and English, there was also a substantial collection of works by German practitioners, who were renowned for combining Mesmer's philosophy with that of Emmanuel Swedenborg; I observed monumental works by Johannes Lavater and Friedrich Hufeland. The only Swedenborgian text I had read myself, I confess, was Balzac's mystically-inclined *Séraphita*, which seemed to me to be one of

the least of the great man's works.

In connection with what I knew about Chapelain's mesmeric experiments, I also paid close attention to a particular piece of furniture with which the room was equipped: a kind of divan with an inclined head-rest, with a stool positioned beside in such a way that a practitioner seated on the stool could comfortably perform mesmeric passes over a patient lying on the divan, and communicate with him—or, more likely, her—with conspiratorial ease. It was, in effect, a station designed for what the pedantic Dupin insisted on calling somniloquism.

No surgery had ever been conducted in the study, to judge by the evidence, but experiments in anesthesia were by no means the only kind currently being conducted by the pioneers of the new science, especially those of a spiritualist persuasion, and speculation was running wild as to what kinds of information might be obtained from sufficiently sensitive somniloquist "mediums". Even physiologists, it was said, believed that information derived by somniloquism could be useful in diagnosis, and spiritualists of a bolder stripe hoped that such mediums might function as oracles dispensing information regarding the future, and the keys to all manner of magical practices and powers. I had no idea, as yet, where Chapelain stood in the magnetic civil war, but I assumed that Dupin's good opinion probably implied that he was at least an agnostic in the tenor of his enquiries.

Chapelain greeted Dupin in a friendly but slightly distant manner, as befit a casual acquaintance who was not a regular guest in his home. He did not seem as surprised as Dupotet had been when Dupin told him that we were making enquiries into the non-arrival of Robert Collyer, but that was only to be expected.

It was obvious that Chapelain was not the person who had sent Ewelina Hanska scurrying to see us. "She is probably anxious about Monsieur Balzac's health," he remarked, when Dupin told him that she had put us on the trail, and that she had seemed rather disturbed. "She has taken full responsibility for

his physical and psychological well-being, you know—a difficult commission, I fear. I have been able to do something for him, on occasion, but it's no secret, alas, that he's a rather difficult patient."

"His working habits are rumored to be direly unhealthy," Dupin agreed. "But he's a genius, after all, and men of genius are often deeply committed to their foibles. If he believes that his way of working is the only one that works for him, he will not abandon it merely because it threatens to be the death of him. He is also said to be relentless in his hopeful search for some elixir that might alleviate his pains in a quasi-magical fashion. Magnetic sleep presumably has not answered his need thus far—but he must have high hopes of Collyer's consignment, to have made Madame Hanska so anxious to obtain news of it."

"So it seems," Chapelain agreed. "I fear that I might be partly responsible for that, albeit unwittingly. I have read Monsieur Balzac's *Recherche de l'absolu*, and should have taken warning therefrom, but I fear that I might have underestimated his capacity for obsession. Perhaps I should not have acquainted him with the more elaborate account of the Valdemar experiment that was sent to me by Nathaniel Falconer, but he had read Edgar Poe's version, and was extremely enthusiastic to know what truth there might be in it. I suppose I could have told him that it was a mere horror story, wholly invented, but I do not like to lie—and to tell the truth, I took some pride and delight in being party to the tale, suspecting that I might be the only man in Paris who was."

As he concluded this speech he looked sharply at Dupin, posing an unspoken question. Dupin nodded his head, a trifle sadly. "It might have been better," he said, "if you *were* the only man in Paris who is acquainted with the fuller story—or if the only other one were Dupotet."

It was Chapelain's turn to nod his head sadly. "I fear that Dupotet has been keeping strange company of late," he said. "Have you been to see him?"

"Yes—but that may have done more harm than good. It had not occurred to him that there might be anything sinister in Collyer's delay, because he did not know that Collyer would be carrying a valuable package, and he has now set off on an investigation of his own."

"Has he gone to see Valdemar's daughter?"

"He has gone to look for her—but Madame Hanska hinted that she might not be at home at present." Dupin's eyes strayed to the divan. "Have you attempted to test Mademoiselle Valdemar's powers?"

"Yes, I have," Chapelain confirmed. "In a spirit of objectivity, of course—but if she's a fraud, she's a very convincing one. I don't wonder that she's taken Dupotet in, if that's what has happened, but it's a damnable shame if she's driven him into the clutches of the Harmonic Society. He promised to be the best of us all. Have you seen him work with Cloquet?"

"Yes, once or twice—but if what I saw this morning is any guide, that kind of collaboration might have become impossible in any public arena. I can understand Dupotet's rancor, if he is nowadays subjected to that kind of hounding on a regular basis. I know that he was deeply disappointed when the findings of the commission of enquiry in which he took part back in 1826 were suppressed, and then censored—twenty years of that kind of frustration might grind anyone down. You must have the patience of a saint to have endured it."

"I no longer try to work in that bear-pit at the Saltpêtrière—but you must not give me too much credit, Monsieur Dupin. I know that you are firmly committed to the physiologist cause yourself, and I have to confess that I have no such commitment."

"Even so, you've avoided the silly practices and intrigues of the Harmonic Society. It will be a tragedy if Dupotet falls prey to them. Mesmerism might survive decades of public derision, provided that its practitioners soldier on regardless, but it cannot survive a mass retreat into calculated esotericism. Forgive me, Monsieur Chapelain, but time might be short—will you tell me what you told Balzac about the American experiment? I've read

Poe's version, of course, but I'd appreciate a fuller account."

Chapelain only hesitated momentarily, and not because he was reluctant to tell his story. "Do you really think that Robert has come to harm?" he asked.

"I don't know. I hope not—but I dare not neglect the possibility, given that…."

"Given that Saint-Germain might be behind it," Chapelain finished for him. "I understand. I've always believed that he's mad rather than evil—but that might only serve to make him more dangerous, especially now that he seems to have the whole Society in his grip."

"Quite so," Dupin agreed. "The experiment…?"

"Of course. The Poe version gives the broad outlines, of course, but is abridged in two respects. The witness who gave the story to Poe was only present for part of the time during the experiment's latter phases—inevitably, since the three colleagues had to work in shifts, around the clock, for several months. Poe's version represents the others as orthodox physicians rather than mesmerists, but that was because he wanted to do his utmost to preserve their anonymity. Had he identified his Dr. D— as a mesmerist, it would have been easy enough to guess that he must be Andrew Davis. Falconer is not so well-known, but the number of New York mesmerists whose names begin with the letter F is rather restricted. The truth is that Poe's carefully-unnamed narrator was the least of the three, although he was the one who induced the state of magnetic sleep in Valdemar, and he tried thereafter to discourage Davis and Falconer from attempting experiments that he was reluctant to undertake. Like me, they had read Lavater and Hufeland, and they were interested in the visionary potential of the sleep phase, while Poe's friend is a physiologist."

"But Poe is a spiritualist," I put in. "He published an account of mesmeric revelations of a cosmic nature in '44, although he later dismissed it as a hoax, as is his wont when people begin to ask too many questions. He tells me that he is planning to write an account of the cosmos based in visionary testimony." Neither

of my interlocutors took any notice of this helpful insertion.

"The physiologist's reluctance, however, only prompted Davis and Falconer to make their attempts to elicit somniloquistic revelations from Valdemar without fully informing their colleague as to what they were doing," Chapelain continued. "While Poe's friend was primarily interested to see how long his patient might remain arrested on the threshold of death, and did not want to risk disturbing that suspension by any suggestion that might provoke a fatal awakening, Davis and Falconer were, so to speak, more interested in the view from that threshold."

"Ah!" sighed Dupin, as if to say: *I thought so*. For myself, mention of the word "threshold" merely instigated a slight psychic twinge. My nightmare still had a tenuous hook in my waking consciousness.

"There is, of course, no guarantee as to the authenticity of what the somniloquist said, when questioned," Chapelain went on, "nor even in the coincidence that what he saw had been reported before. Indeed, the fact that Valdemar had almost certainly read Bulwer's *Zanoni* makes it highly likely that what he said was a distorted memory of what he had read in the novel, rather than an actual experience. Are you familiar with the work, Monsieur Dupin?"

This time, the twinge was more like an electric shock—but I told myself that Chapelain's citation of the title could only be a coincidence, and not an improbable one, given that there could be very few literate men interested in occult themes who had not read *Zanoni* within the last thirty months. Nevertheless, it was with a definite feeling of gloomy apprehension that I heard my friend's reply.

"I am," Dupin confirmed, furrowing his brow in a manner suggestive of the fact that he too found the coincidence disturbing. "Indeed, I had a dream only last night in which its substance featured in a somewhat nightmarish fashion."

CHAPTER SIX
Valdemar's Vision

"In that case," Chapelain continued, with what now seemed to be a dire inevitability, "you will doubtless remember the description of the Dweller of the Threshold: the entity with the blazing eyes that Glyndon encounters after disobeying Mejnour's instructions?"

"I do. It is, alas, one of the most memorable passages in the literature of the present decade. Are you telling me that Valdemar reported to his eager listeners that he had had a vision of the Dweller of the Threshold?"

"So he said—but unlike Glyndon in the novel, he did not swoon at the sight of her, and even went so far as to supply the kiss that she demanded from him. Indeed, he reported that he obtained a valuable gift from that kiss, of a sort better than any that Zanoni had previously obtained from his initiation into the Rosicrucian mysteries, but which might be available to any would-be initiate who had the courage and psychic acumen to recover it by a similar means, rather than taking the long way round."

I frowned, because that did not seem to tally with the implications of Bulwer's text—but then I shook my head, remembering that we were, after all, dealing with the power of suggestion exercised within a dream...assuming that whatever Valdemar had been experiencing in his death-defying magnetic sleep had been subject to the perverse logic of dreams rather than the stern demands of reason.

If Dupin was finding echoes of his own nightmare in what Chapelain was telling him, he gave no formal indication of it. "A gift akin to the elixir of life, do you mean?" he asked, calmly.

"Yes—but not in the form of a potion or a powder, as legend so often represents that alchemical treasure…and as Monsieur Balzac represents it himself, in the sarcastic satires that do not entirely mask his fascination with the notion."

"What form, then?" Dupin wanted to know.

"According to the paraphrase of Valdemar's testimony that Falconer sent to me, what is involved in the cultivation of human longevity—not immortality, which is a divine attribute, but a powerful resistance to all illness, including the aging process — is a kind of psychically-induced metamorphosis, brought about by the power of the suitably-informed will. It cannot guarantee that a man might live forever, even if properly and fully obtained, for the body still remains vulnerable to violent death, and to the weakening effects of certain sentiments. Rigid asceticism, it seems, is one of the requirements of the alchemical transformation. The most intriguing aspect of Valdemar's testimony, however—whether or not it is a confabulation—was his insistence that there is an effect of contagion associated to the metamorphosis in question: that it affects not only the primary recipient of the gift, but those with whom he is closely associated, at least to the extent that they can participate in his self-discipline and share his philosophical attitude. Nat Falconer commented that this might help to explain why reputed mages routinely gather groups of fanatical acolytes around them, who are convinced that closeness to their spiritual leader might result in a measured transfer of his superiority to them. It is, of course, very much in the interests of such poseurs to convince their followers of the reality of some such contagion…."

"As Saint-Germain has undoubtedly done in the bosom of the Harmonic Society," Dupin said, thoughtfully. "And it is, I suppose, a contagious agent of this kind that someone believes to be in Collyer's possession? Someone, that is, who might have set out to rob him in the course of his journey from London to

Paris"

"*Believes* might be too strong a word," Chapelain suggested. "The mere possibility would be enough to motivate a man of a certain dubious stripe. Such talismans can be useful, even if they have no real effect—like the relics of saints. If experiments in animal magnetism have demonstrated nothing else, they have certainly left no doubt as to the awesome power of suggestion."

"Indeed," Dupin agreed. "And I presume that the supposed magic agent in question comprises what Dupotet called Valdemar's *mortal remains*?"

"That's the other respect in which Poe's version of the experiment is incomplete," Chapelain confirmed. "As a writer of horror stories whose tales are explicitly contrived to work towards shocking endings, Poe naturally wanted the ending of his narrative to be as succinct as possible, so he was content to describe what happened to Valdemar, once he was released from his suspended animation, as an abrupt decay into loathsome liquid putrescence. According to Falconer, the process was not so rapid, and not so simple. The relative slowness of the event is probably insignificant, but there is one aspect of the complication that might be—or, at least, might be thus construed by an interested party."

He paused for dramatic effect, waiting for a prompt. Dupin would undoubtedly have provided it, but my patience was wearing thin, and I had been waiting for an opportunity to interrupt.

"But all this is absurd!" I protested. "It's manifestly ridiculous! It certainly seems to me that whatever Valdemar is supposed to have learned from the magical kiss that he supposedly bestowed upon the fiery-eyed Dweller of the Threshold, the last thing it could be is the secret of an elixir of life, given that, as soon as he was released from his magnetic sleep, he began to rot—however rapidly or slowly that process took effect. Whether Poe's account is faulty or not, the fact surely remains that Valdemar was already beyond the threshold of death when he had his supposed vision, and that there was no

way back for him. All that your three colleagues contrived to do, Dr. Chapelain, was to delay his decay for a while. I don't call *that* an elixir of life."

"Nor do I, to be honest," Chapelain replied, equably, "but Falconer was not so sure—nor, when I told him the tale, was Honoré de Balzac."

"You should not underestimate the magnitude of the experiment's achievement, my friend," Dupin put in, quietly. "We are not talking about a matter of hours or days, remember, but of seven months. Whatever metamorphosis was wrought in Valdemar's body, whether it was simply by virtue of the suggestion implanted by the magnetizer, or by virtue of some transcendental experience that Valdemar was able to undergo on his own behalf, the preservation of a measure of life within the body of a man who was undoubtedly dead is no small achievement."

"If legend can be trusted," Chapelain added, "the phenomenon of uncanny preservation might not be unique, but it might be significant that the same decay-resisting faculty is mainly credited to saints of an unusually ascetic stripe. Not that I make any claim to the accuracy of such legends, of course—I merely observe the existence of the allegations."

"Very scrupulous, I'm sure," I said, "but the fact remains that Valdemar did die, perhaps rather horribly. I cannot see that he can have obtained the slightest joy, or any other privilege, from his protracted semi-existence, and nor could Poe. Unless I'm missing something, I cannot see why anyone would be interested in any contagion that might or might not be contained in his mortal remains."

"There is a piece of the puzzle of which you're not yet aware, my friend," Dupin put in. "In case you had forgotten, we were suspended in something of a dramatic pause when you interrupted. Dr. Chapelain was about to reveal the other detail omitted from Poe's account: the *complication*, as he put it."

Chapelain smiled. "I did pause for dramatic effect," he admitted. "Balzac is not the only story-teller among my clients.

Perhaps such devices are unworthy of me, as a scrupulous man of science, so I shall state the missing fact as brutally as I can: the liquid residue that Poe describes as a product of putrescence was slightly luminous."

"Ah!" said Dupin. "I see: the so-called phosphorescence of putrescence, to borrow a poetic phrase."

Chapelain had a pedantic steak too, though, and he was quick to offer a correction. "Not exactly," he said. "I am familiar with phosphorescence, as is Falconer, and the phosphorescence associated with the decay of living tissue tends to be tinted green. This was allegedly a purer and whiter glow. Falconer did not say so, but it sounds to me more akin to the kind of bioluminescence associated with glow-worms and certain…."

"The stuff of haloes," Dupin murmured, following his own train of thought and cutting through Chapelain's. "Or, at least, something that might be mistaken for the stuff of haloes. We are well used to connecting light with life—especially supernatural life. There is nothing very much that such light might do for a man who is already a corpse, I suppose, unless perhaps he were heaven-bound—but for a man still living, luminosity of that supposedly-magical sort might be a powerful psychological lure, of which he might expect great things…especially if he had the mystical turn of mind of a Balzac, or a Saint-Germain, rather than the sternly rational mind of a scientist, like you or I."

The *you* was probably directed at Chapelain, but I took the liberty of including myself in the generalization. I was, apparently, the only one clear-headed and commonsensical enough to see how utterly ridiculous this whole thing was. Bulwer's Rosicrucian balderdash had certainly caught the popular imagination, but not to any good effect.

"I'm sorry," Chapelain said, "if my indiscretion has caused trouble—especially if anything has happened to Robert."

"Was it you who told Madame Hanska that Collyer was bringing the consignment to Paris?" Dupin was quick to ask.

"No—I didn't know that that until you told me, and I'm slightly surprised to hear that Davis allowed Valdemar's

remains to be removed from New York. I merely told Balzac and Madame Hanska the expanded version of Valdemar's story, as it was told to me."

"In that case, the most that your indiscretion has achieved is to excite Balzac and Madame Hanska," Dupin assured him. "Someone else must have told Madame Hanska, or Balzac, about Collyer—almost certainly Mademoiselle Valdemar. Saint-Germain and the Harmonic Society must have their own informational channels—unless her anxiety regarding the possibility of their intervention results from her own indiscretion. If Falconer communicated his impressions to you, though, Davis might well have communicated his to presumed sharers in his so-called harmonial philosophy. At any rate, if any harm has come to Collyer, you are not in any way to blame. What we have to do now, I think, is to figure out exactly how Mademoiselle Valdemar fits into the puzzle. She is, of course, her father's legitimate heir, but there seems to be more to her involvement than that."

"If she's genuine," Chapelain said, "then she's a remarkably powerful medium—perhaps the most powerful in Paris. If, on the other hand, she's tied up in some way with Saint-Germain…."

"There does seem to be a pattern forming," Dupin observed, mournfully, "whereby allegedly-sensitive young females are being routinely taken up by male manipulators, who control their visions…or their impostures. Your science has its seamier side, alas."

"Even Elliotson seems to have fallen prey to temptations of that sort," the doctor observed, effortlessly matching Dupin's tone. "I fear that his erotic exploits virtually issued an open invitation to Wakley and *The Lancet* to pursue and discredit him—although similar temptations are set before us all, and can be hard to resist. There's no future for poor Elliotson now, in London at least, and he might well have inflicted mortal injury on the cause of magnetic healing in England. We live in troubled times, Monsieur Dupin. There's Revolution in the air,

politically as well as scientifically, but I fear that both its aspects might lead to disaster rather than rational reform."

Dupin stood up, evidently satisfied that he had all the information that Chapelain could provide.

"Thank you, Doctor," he said. "You've been extremely helpful—unlike Dupotet…and, I fear, Madame Hanska, in spite of the effort she put into ensuring my involvement."

"I'm glad to be of service," Chapelain said. "Especially if there's still time to help Robert, should he need help. You will let me know how it all comes out, won't you?"

"Of course," Dupin assured him—and we took our leave.

"What now?" I asked, as we searched for a fiacre. "The Prefecture?"

"We don't have enough time for that," he said, consulting his pocket-watch. "In any case, Chapelain's testimony suggests more promising lines of enquiry. We shall go back to your home, to discover what has transpired while we have carefully left the house empty."

"You mean," I said, fearfully, "that you think it might have been invaded by robbers searching for Collyer's package?"

"I certainly hope so," he said. "That was the whole point of vacating it. How else were we to tempt our adversaries to tip their hand? With luck, we might even be able to count them, and measure their strength."

CHAPTER SEVEN
An Unexpected Turn of Events

When the cab dropped us at the corner of the Boulevard, Dupin made off yet again, seemingly in a desperate hurry to speak to one of the *gamins* who are ever-present in the streets of Paris. The two of them engaged in a rapid and hushed conversation, whose substance did not seem to be at all to Dupin's liking, although I saw him give the lad forty sous—forty sous that he could, had he been so inclined, have used to pay our cab fares for a whole day of hectic activity.

When I caught up with him, he was frowning deeply.

"Has that urchin been watching my house?" I demanded. "Are you mad, to inform a wretch of that sort that the house is empty? He could easily have summoned a dozen of his disreputable friends and ransacked the place."

"He's not a thief but a *mouche*," Dupin old me, distractedly, "and his friends are all busy, either on similar sentry-duty, or following Dupotet."

Mouche—fly, in English—was the name popularly given to errand-boys of a particular sort, who were hired by police inspectors to carry out surveillance work for them. Dupin obviously thought that Madame Hanska's ban on police involvement only extended to accredited officers of the law.

"Oh, very well," I said. "I presume from your expression that Collyer has not turned up, nor any would-be robbers."

"My young colleague was not able to identify any of the callers at our residence, although he was able to furnish me with

descriptions. What troubles me is that both the callers who were seen to arrive, at an unsociably early hour, rang the doorbell and waited, like respectable callers—*and that both were let in.*"

"By whom?" I demanded, outraged.

"The woman, who arrived first, was admitted by a man, and the man, who arrived second, was admitted by the woman. The woman and the man who had let her in were then seen to leave, together, in something of a hurry, closing the door behind them."

I took a moment or two to digest the implications of this welter of data. "You mean," I said, eventually, "that the second of the callers who rang the bell—the second man—is still inside?"

"Apparently so. What mystifies me, however, is how the man who opened the door to the woman got in without being seen for my *mouche* is no fool, and he has had all the entrances covered since eight. Which suggests...."

"I don't believe in magical translocations," I told him.

"Nor do I," he said. "Which suggests, as I was saying, that he was already in the house when we left, having got in while you were asleep. Oh, what a fool I am! I knew that there was something strange about that mulled wine you gave me. Your surprise ingredient wouldn't, by any chance, have been opium?"

"Certainly not," I said. "I bought the mixture at my local herbalist's, as usual—but he did tell me that it was a new blend. Now I think about it, he was very insistent that I ought to try it last night. He's a good man, though, in spite of his profession—it's unthinkable that he could have been guilty of any malicious intent."

"Perhaps it is," Dupin said, eyeing my front door speculatively, from a respectable distance. "But is it unthinkable, I wonder, that he might have been subject to some kind of mesmeric suggestion? Chapelain assures me that such suggestions can be planted, to take effect hours, or even days, later—long after the subject has been woken up from his magnetic sleep."

"Much as a nightmare can sometimes continue to irritate you long after the sleep that brought it has been dispelled," I

muttered.

Dupin did not appear to pay any heed to that remark. Instead, he said: "Take out your key, my friend, and let us in to your house—but let's go carefully, in case there's an opportunity to surprise someone...or, at least, to avoid being taken by surprise by someone lying in ambush."

I did as I was told. We tiptoed to the door, and I turned the key in the lock as quietly as possible. Then we tiptoed along the hallway.

As things turned out, our precautions were needless. There was, indeed, someone in the house—but he was lying on the hearth-rug in front of the sitting-room fire, quite unconscious. The hearth-rug was, alas, none too clean, and I dreaded to think what continued exposure to it might be doing to the poor fellow's sumptuous black frock-coat and neatly-pressed trousers. My first impression of him, drawn from his costume, was that he was something of a dandy.

As soon as he saw the supine dandy, Dupin groaned. I could tell that, whoever the unlucky visitor was, he was not on Dupin's hastily-compiled mental list of people he might expect to find in that situation.

"Do you know who that is?" I asked him, in a whisper—although I had not the slightest reason to be fearful that I might awaken my unwelcome guest.

"I fear so," Dupin confirmed. "And his presence here, in this rather ignominious predicament, throws all my calculations out. I shall have to begin all over again in the attempt to fathom this ridiculous business."

I was glad to hear him call it ridiculous, but annoyed by his failure to provide a name. "Well, who is it?" I demanded, waspishly.

"This," said Dupin, tiredly, "is the man that I had mistakenly assumed to be behind all this chicanery, but who now appears to be yet another investigator trying to catch up with the runaway course of events. What name he was given by his doubtless loving parents, I don't know, but nowadays he calls himself the

Comte de Saint-Germain. As I explained to you a little while ago, he is a self-styled Rosicrucian, and the recently-elected President of the Philosophical Harmonic Society of Paris."

He knelt down beside the supine body, but immediately snatched his head backwards, apparently having encountered a noxious odor near to floor-level.

"Ether," he said. "Now, that *is* an ironic twist."

I remembered that he had used the word before. "What on Earth is ether?" I demanded.

"The substance that will probably render the debate regarding the efficacy of mesmeric anesthesia irrelevant," he said. "A powerful chemical anesthetic. Its effect was discovered long ago by Paracelsus, but the medical establishment refused to take it up because they were then waging war against his chemical medicine. Now that they are fighting on a very different front, however, interest in chemical anesthesia has suddenly been revived. Within a year or two, ether and chloroform will both be tested in the operating theater, if only to interrupt the surge of interest in mesmeric anesthesia.[3] Whoever took Saint-Germain by surprise is ahead of the trend—at a guess, I'd say that a rag soaked in the liquid was clamped over his mouth and nose, and he was held tight until the dose took effect. His opponent must have been strong and vigorous...unless, of course, the woman helped."

"I don't understand," I said. "Is this one of the men your street-urchin saw ringing the doorbell?"

"Yes."

"But why was he calling on me, in such a conventional manner? Thus far, you've painted a picture of him as a devious Machiavellian—the sort of person, for instance, who might contrive to dupe a herbalist into selling a mildly narcotic mixture with which to make mulled wine."

---

3. As the reader will undoubtedly be aware, this prediction of Dupin's was fulfilled within a matter of months, and chemical anesthesia enjoyed a wave of fashionability from 1846 onwards that has not yet abated—which did, indeed, put a heavy nail into the coffin of mesmeric anesthesia.

"That's exactly the kind of person he is," Dupin agreed. "And I have not completely set aside the hypothesis that he might be putting on a show, having had himself drugged in order to infiltrate our investigation—but one must always beware of preferring an unlikely explanation to the likeliest one, simply because one is clever enough to perceive it. If he seems to be on the wrong side of the conspiracy in this case, it might well be that he is. If so, I doubt that he knew, any more than Dupotet or Chapelain did, that Collyer was supposed to be delivering Valdemar's remains to you yesterday…if, in fact, Collyer really was supposed to be doing that…."

"You mean that we might all have been sent off on a wild goose chase?"

"I doubt that—whatever these people are chasing, it's no mere game, and they really do seem to have expected it to be delivered here." He knelt down again, flapping his hand to dispel the last remnants of the lingering odor, and set about trying to rouse his old adversary.

It took time, and some vigorous slapping, but Saint-Germain eventually came round. He was taller than Dupotet, and considerably more handsome, but the apparent innocence of his features meant that he did not look nearly as imposing—until he opened his eyes and focused his stare.

As befit a would-be Rosicrucian magus, Saint-Germain really did have impressive eyes—if not those of a Dweller of the Threshold, at least those of a thoroughly convincing mesmerist.

The dandy sat up, took a few seconds to collect himself, dusted down his coat as best he could, while wrinkling his nose—and then contrived a lazy smile. "I know you don't approve of me, Dupin," he said, "but don't you think that a greeting of this sort is a little beyond the social pale. We're civilized men, after all—and I did ring the bell, as any honest visitor would."

"It wasn't me who drugged you!" Dupin objected.

"Oh," said the stricken man, not yet attempting to rise to his feet. His gaze automatically transferred itself to me.

"Nor me," I assured him. "It must have been the man who

opened the door to the woman who opened the door to you—unless it was the woman herself."

Saint-German frowned in puzzlement as he strove to track the intricacies of the sentence, and its implications.

"Did you recognize the woman who opened the door?" Dupin put in.

"Of course I did." Saint-Germain replied. "It was Mademoiselle Valdemar. I was not entirely surprised to see her, since I knew her to be an interested party, although I had certainly not expected her to get here ahead of me. Whoever put the wad of German tinder over my face took me from behind, while she was still standing before me, seemingly as innocent as a lamb—but I suppose she must have been a party to the attack, if only an unwitting or reluctant one. She has been quite generous of late in offering her services to experimenters. The man who drugged me might, I suppose, have been Chapelain."

"It was not," said Dupin, firmly. "We can vouch for that, as he can for us. Can you vouch for Dupotet?"

Saint-Germain wrinkled his nose. "I believe so," he said. "He would have needed to move very rapidly indeed to get here ahead of me—and he did seem genuinely surprised by what you had told him. Were they lying in wait for *you*, do you suppose? Did I fall into a trap set for you, and scare them off on your behalf?"

"I don't know," Dupin said. Reluctantly, he offered the sitting man his arm, in order that he might haul himself to his feet. Then the two of them stood looking at one another, as if they were wondering whether or not to engage in a staring match. They were exactly the same height, but their eyes were contrasting, Dupin's pale brown irises seeming much less naturally intimidating than Saint-Germain's near-black ones. Eventually, the tacit truce held, and they decided that wary co-operation was preferable to proud combat, at least for the time being.

"If they weren't lying in wait," Saint-Germain continued, as if thinking aloud, "then they were looking for something—except that, if you two actually had Valdemar's supposed mortal

remains in your possession, you'd hardly have left them lying around in a desk-drawer, would you?"

"No," I confirmed, although the question was presumably rhetorical.

"Which leaves us with the three questions in dire need of answers. Where is Collyer? What has he brought with him from England, if anything? And what on Earth is Mademoiselle Valdemar playing at?"

I knew that Saint-Germain was trying to provoke a reaction from Dupin, but I knew my friend too well to be anxious that he might obtain one—and he did not. Instead, Dupin sat him down and poured him a glass of brandy. Saint-Germain sniffed it suspiciously, but apparently found its odor inoffensive, and took a sip.

"You thought I was behind this, didn't you, Dupin?" Saint-German resumed, as the brandy warmed his throat. "I'm flattered—I wish I were. Unfortunately, I suspect that someone might be trying to put one over on the Harmonic Society. You've heard about the bait, I suppose—from Chapelain if not from Madame Hanska. Absurd, no? What do they take us for, Dupin?"

"Absurd," Dupin agreed, in a neutral tone.

"When it comes to elixirs of life," Saint-German added, "I'm a seller, not a buyer. Poe and Bulwer have a lot to answer for—they're cheapening the whole game, you know, by turning it into the stuff of *feuilletons*. I'd gladly strangle the pair of them."

"So you don't believe that the liquid residue of Valdemar's posthumous metamorphosis has any magical properties?" Dupin asked, mildly, as if to make certain that Saint-Germain really was the mountebank he assumed him to be.

Under other circumstances, I presumed, Saint-Germain might have been determined to maintain his pose as an earnest Rosicrucian and powerful mage at all costs, but for the moment, his guard was down, and he obviously knew that Dupin was not a man to be easily fooled.

"Of course not," the dandy replied. "This is some kind of

confidence-trick. Can you imagine that Davis would have let the stuff out of his custody if he'd thought for a moment that it had any magical power? Indeed, if the tale of its faint luminosity is true, I can't believe that he would have surrendered it at all, although I suppose he might have been forced by his collaborators to agree to divide the sample in three. Why would either of the others send his share to Mademoiselle Valdemar, though? And why use Collyer as a courier? Someone is trying to play both of us for fools, Dupin. We can't tolerate that, can we? We might not like one another, but it's not in my interest to have your intelligence insulted, any more than it's in yours to have mine insulted, else our ongoing rivalry might come to be reckoned a mere contest of clods."

"You're proposing, then, that we work together to solve the problem?" Dupin said, arching an eyebrow.

"Why, yes," said the impostor—and then groaned. "Oh, come on! You don't think I staged all of this, do you? You can't imagine that I had myself drugged in order to worm my way into your good books! I suppose I ought to be flattered, but there are limits…."

"As a matter of fact," Dupin said, "I do believe you—if only because your overweening pride is so great that you would never have conceded so easily that you might need my help to fathom this mystery. That does not, however, mean that I'm willing to collaborate with you. You're a charlatan, an opportunist and a petty crook, whose ambitions are purely mercenary."

Saint-Germain went white, and I was fully convinced that he felt deeply insulted by that accusation—so deeply, in fact, that he would not dignify it with a mere denial. "In that case," he said, "I'm sorry for having disturbed you. Working together, we would have been more knowledgeable and more adept than we shall be if we are forced to work separately, but if that is what you prefer…."

At that point in the conversation, I might have been inclined to attempt diplomacy, but Dupin was always a sterner man than I am. Besides, he had the utmost faith in his own powers of

reasoning, and would never have conceded that he might need help in solving a problem of logic. It was, in the end, Saint-Germain who hesitated, as he picked up his hat, gloves and cane in the hallway, and opted to make a gesture of compromise. "Do *you* know who it was that knocked me out?" he could not resist asking of Dupin.

"No," Dupin replied. "But you may be sure that I shall find out."

"Not if I get to Mademoiselle Valdemar before you do," the President of the Harmonic society retorted.

"If you harm a hair on the young lady's head," Dupin warned him, "I'll see to it that you reap the wages of the sin."

Saint-Germain laughed as I opened the door to let him out. "Don't be such a melodramatic fool, Dupin," he said. "I love *the young lady* with all my heart—she's my star pupil. If she's making some gauche attempt to outwit her master, I admire her for it, and I'll treat her very tenderly when I outwit her. If *you* harm a hair on her head, though, I'll reckon with *you*."

Dupin let him have the last word, and we watched him head for the boulevard, strutting and swinging his cane like a swagger-stick.

"If you don't mind me saying so, my friend," I observed, slipping into my native tongue, "you might have gotten more out of him if you'd handled him with a little more subtlety and politeness."

"I could only have *gotten* more out of him if there was something more to be *gotten*," Dupin observed, mimicking my American accent and style of speech before reverting to his own language. "But I did obtain one interesting item of information."

"What's that?"

"That he does not think of himself entirely as a charlatan. Like many a trickster, he has fallen for what you would probably call *his own line of patter*. Success has gone to his head, and in becoming President of the Harmonic Society, he has begun to think of himself as a real magus, even though he cannot believe that the potion Collyer was carrying is magical, or that

Mademoiselle Valdemar's powers are authentic. If Dupotet really has become involved with him, theirs is likely to be a *folie à deux*."

"Like Mejnour and Zanoni," I suggested, a trifle provocatively.

He looked at me curiously. "Your nightmare was similar to the one attributed to Valdemar, was it not?" he asked.

"Yes," I replied, "although it was more faithful to Bulwer's text. Was yours in the same vein?"

"A similar vein," he admitted, "though sufficiently different to be intriguing. You're right to make a point of it—the coincidence is genuinely strange, though not necessarily supernatural. Nor should we be too hasty in writing off *Zanoni* as a mere *feuilleton*, as Saint-Germain just did. It is, at the very least, scrupulously-researched. There are elements of Mejnour's philosophy, as reported in the novel, that are not unconsonant with my own."

"You mean that you believe there might actually be such entities as the Dweller of the Threshold?" I asked, trying to sound incredulous—although I had seen enough during my acquaintance with Dupin to know that there were far more things in heaven and earth than were dreamt of in Auguste Comte's philosophy.

"Even that," he conceded, grudgingly. "But once again, it would be foolish to prefer the unlikely hypothesis to the likeliest one, simply because one is wise enough to perceive it. The first thing we must do now is to try to ascertain whether Mademoiselle Valdemar really is the scheming charlatan that Saint-Germain has just painted for us. I am reluctant to believe it, but the evidence is stacking up...unless, of curse, Saint-Germain is lying."

"But how are we going to find her?" I asked.

"By the only means that has been offered to us. Our expedition to the Prefecture must be postponed again, if not abandoned entirely, and we must take the risk of disturbing Monsieur Balzac, in order that we might ask Madame Hanska the ques-

tions that we did not know enough to ask last night."

And we set off in our turn for the boulevard, in search of yet another cab. I was profoundly grateful that all the snow was gone, and that the roads were clear. The sun had come out too, and the afternoon was not unpleasant.

CHAPTER EIGHT
A Great Man in Dire Straits

Monsieur Balzac, it transpired, was not hard at work on the latest segment of the *Comédie humaine*, although he would dearly have liked to be. He was, in fact, in bed, apparently very ill, and in evident fear of his life.

Had I been in such a state, I would have refused all visitors, and perhaps Balzac would have done likewise—although he was rumored to be a man who was ever fond of complaining at length about his ills to anyone prepared to listen—but Madame Hanska gave him no chance to decline to receive us. She seemed to be anxious to let us see her lover's plight, in order that we might better appreciate the magnitude of the problem that she had set for us. Dupin, I think, might have been willing to settle for talking to her in a sitting-room, in view of Balzac's indisposition, but she wasted no time in ushering us into the author's bedroom and introducing us to him.

In all fairness, the great man did seem glad that we had come, and eager to hear our news. He tried to prop himself up on his elbow, but could not do it, and was obviously annoyed his failure. "Have you found him?" he asked, in a conspicuously weak voice.

"We have not yet ascertained Dr. Collyer's whereabouts," Dupin admitted, "nor the whereabouts of the package he was supposed to be carrying, if it is no longer in his possession. We need more information if we are to proceed productively, with all due haste. It's imperative that we speak to Mademoiselle

Valdemar. Can you tell us where she is, Madame Hanska?"

Ewelina Hanska shook her head, a trifle indecisively. "She gave me the strictest instruction that she was only to be contacted if and when you had obtained Robert Collyer's package. She fears that she might be in danger from the people who might have contrived to intercept it."

"I do understand that," Dupin assured her, "and I understand your reluctance to break a promise, but…."

"Tell the fellow what he wants to know, Evy." Balzac grunted, without attempting to raise his head from his pillow.

The great author was obviously not looking his best, but I could not help thinking that he seemed to be a remarkably ugly man, and wondering exactly what Madame Hanska saw in him. I knew that they had first become acquainted by letter, while she was still married, and that she had been moved to write to him by reading his works—works whose genius was, of course, entirely independent of his unprepossessing appearance. It did seem to me, however, that she must be an unusually stern-minded woman to have allowed her admiration for his genius to have over-ridden such factors as his dire appearance when she had decided, following her husband's death, to devote herself entirely to the author's intimate care.

Dupin turned his attention back to the man on the bed. "I hope that you won't mind my asking, Monsieur Balzac," he said, "but how did you make the acquaintance of Mademoiselle Valdemar?"

Balzac opened his mouth to answer, but was interrupted by a fit of coughing, and Madame Hanska was quick to step in. "Polish exiles in Paris form a close-knit community," she said. "We are all fervent nationalists, of course, united in our hatred of Russian imperialism—which creates a bond of intense fellow-feeling between us. Mademoiselle Valdemar and I had a mutual acquaintance in Dr. Chapelain, and she had heard of Monsieur Balzac's poor health—and also his lack of success in finding appropriate treatment. She is, as you must know, a powerful medium. She volunteered her assistance. Although

she is not a physician, she felt that her talents might be useful, in matters of diagnosis if not in curative terms."

"So she has been entranced in this very room—beside Monsieur Balzac's sick-bed? Was it Dr. Chapelain who put her to sleep?"

"No—she no longer has any need of a mesmerist, having become able to enter into the state of magnetic sleep at will. She did her work alone."

"Alone? Do you mean that even you were not present?"

"Not always. Sometimes, she felt that my presence was distracting—but she always repeated to me, afterwards, what her visions had revealed."

"And did they reveal that the contents of Robert Collyer's package might be effective in treating Monsieur Balzac's condition?"

"Oh, by no means! We reached that conclusion independently, by combining the story that Dr. Chapelain told us with her observations as to the nature and seriousness of Honoré's condition, the spiritual component of which defies all herbal or chemical remedy. We know, of course, how valuable Dr. Collyer's cargo is, and how much demand will be placed upon it even by the honest experimenters who are waiting for it, but… well, I hope you will forgive me, Monsieur Dupin, but this is *Honoré de Balzac*—the greatest writer in France, who lives in mortal dread of dying before he can complete his grand plan for the *Comédie humaine*. Can you blame me for wanting to advance his claim ahead of so many others? Can you blame me for my sense of urgency, my desperation, when I came to see you last night, after Jana let it slip that Collyer seemed to have been delayed?"

Dupin politely refrained from pointing out that Balzac was only the second greatest writer in France—which hardly mattered much, since France had more than its fair share of the world's great writers, all of whom were worth any effort to conserve their genius. Had we been talking about the greatest writer in Poland, it might have been a different matter. "I do

understand, Madame," is what my friend actually said, "and I do sympathize." He turned back to the invalid, however, to ask his next question. "Monsieur Balzac," he said, in what can only be described as a melodramatic whisper, *"have you seen the Dweller of the Threshold?"*

Balzac was in no fit condition to go pale; the redness in his face was not the kind that can be wiped away by a temporary constriction of the carotid artery. Nor was there much margin to allow him to seem in greater torment that he already was. He did react, however, and although his lips formed no coherent syllable, I was in no doubt that his response was affirmative.

Madame Hanska seemed annoyed that the question had been asked, let alone answered, but Dupin turned back to her with a remarkable swiftness. "Have no fear, Madame," he said. "I understand the consequences of my question very fully, for I have experienced similar visions myself. I have also read the *Harmonies de l'enfer*, for which you have been combing the banks of the Seine, and some of the texts you obtained in its stead. I make no claim to be an adept, but I am well-versed in these matters, and I am aware of the true consequences of the principle of plenitude."

Madame Hanska was nodding, but there was wariness in her expression as well as relief. "Then providence was on my side when I found you last night as a guest in your friend's house," she said. "You understand what is at stake here."

"Yes," Dupin said, "I do."

"Do you believe that Robert Collyer has been intercepted, and his package stolen?"

"Yes," said Dupin, again, "I do."

"Do you know by whom?"

"No—but I have a strong suspicion. In order to confirm or negate that suspicion, it's imperative that I see Mademoiselle Valdemar as soon as possible. Will you—knowing, as you do, what is at stake—take the chance of entrusting me with information as to her whereabouts?"

I could see that Madame Hanska's conscience was still inhib-

iting her—but once again, the man on the bed, who clearly believed that he was in imminent danger of death, said: "Tell the fellow what he wants to know. If he's a villain, so much the worse—but even that rogue Vidocq paints him as a saint, and we have no choice but to trust *someone*."

"Very well," said Madame Hanska—who, I suspected, could resist anything and anyone except for the man to whom she had dedicated her life. "I'll tell you where Jana can be found—but you must not tell another soul, and you must show the utmost discretion in going there. In addition to the agents of the Harmonic Society, Russian spies are everywhere, and since the Cracow rising…well, suffice it to say that if you were to be followed…."

"I'm aware of the dangers," Dupin assured her, "and I have the skill to evade Russian spies, as well as any hirelings that Monsieur Saint-Germain might entrust with that task."

Madame Hanska did not seem surprised by the citation of Saint-Germain's name, nor by the omission therefrom of the honorific *particule*, which even she only added to Balzac's name when making formal declarations. She knew and understood how common it was for men to make tacit claims to aristocratic descent purely for the purpose of cultivating an image.

She did not have to ask me for a piece of paper this time, and had steel nibs a-plenty ready to hand—but when she had written down an address and shown it to Dupin, she immediately set fire to the piece of paper with the nearest candle-flame, and held it in such a manner as to ensure its consumption.

Dupin nodded, as if in approval of the melodramatic gesture. "I am very glad to have met you, sir," he said to the stricken author, "and wish with all my heart that I had done so in better circumstances—but I swear that I shall do my best to procure you the cure that you need. Trust me, I beg you."

"Thank you," said Balzac, in a stage-whisper.

"You have my thanks too, sirs," said Madame Hanska. "May God go with you, and protect you."

Dupin's answering bow as more than usually solemn, and

his face seemed very stern indeed as we hurried down the stairs and left the house.

For once, we did not hail a cab, and Dupin looked around continually as we walked through the mazy streets surrounding Balzac's home. I assumed that he was on the lookout for anyone who might be following us—and so he was, in a manner of speaking, but it turned out that he was looking for a friend rather than an enemy. Eventually, the *gamin* that he had earlier spoken to outside my house poked his head over a nearby wall and hissed like a cat. Dupin rushed to speak to him, carefully and insistently—but he did so in a whisper so faint that I could hardly hear a word of what he said, although I caught the names of Dupotet and Chapelain. Then the boy vanished again, and Dupin was quick to resume his steady march.

By now, I was looking round myself, fearful of Russians and mesmerists alike. The sun sets early in February, and it was already reddening in the west, painting a few fugitive clouds with eerie shades of pink and purple.

"Come on!" Dupin urged. "We must move quickly, for this is a race of sorts, even if it is one in which we are intended to finish ahead of the field—but not too quickly, for accurate timing might well make the difference between ultimate success and failure. At the very least, I would hate to disappoint the lady, since she has gone to so much trouble to cast me in her little melodrama—she must be even fonder of the theaters on the Boulevard du Temple than you are!"

CHAPTER NINE
Beyond the Faubourg Saint-Martin

We walked on for some time, at a brisk but unhurried pace, before I finally realized that Dupin had no intention of trying to find a fiacre, even though I could not believe that he thought we were still in danger of pursuit. I was not intimidated by the prospect of a long hike, though; in the early days of our friendship we had often walked for hours on end through the streets of the city—though rarely, I admit, in the months of winter.

"Where are we going?" I eventually asked him, unable to contain my curiosity any longer.

"Through the Faubourg Saint-Martin," was the only immediate answer I got—and a very vague one, for the district in question stretched for miles on end north of the intersection of the eponymous Boulevard and the Boulevard du Temple. We had already passed the Hospice du Nord, so I guessed that we would probably be going through the Barrière de la Villette, into a region where I had never set foot before.

The necessity of giving some sort of answer to my question must have loosened Dupin's tongue, however, for he soon began to speak, and I expressed a silent sigh, in the expectation that my seething curiosity would soon be satisfied.

"For once," he commented, "I have to agree with Saint-Germain. Mademoiselle Valdemar's temerity is admirable, and her attention to detail breathtaking. There is an aesthetic element to this project that almost makes it impossible to view it as a mere crime."

"But Mademoiselle Valdemar *is* a criminal, is she not?" I said, just to make sure. "She really is guilty of the plot that you were initially inclined to attribute to Saint-Germain?"

"She certainly seems to be a villain," Dupin agreed, switching abruptly from taciturnity to loquacity, as he often did once he had sorted out his ideas to his own satisfaction. "Is she a criminal? Yes, I think so—but a criminal of a sort that the law does not yet recognize very clearly, for which reason it might be very difficult to bring her before a tribunal. Now that we have given up burning alleged witches—a measure of which I approve wholeheartedly—we have little legal apparatus left to bring to bear on modern fraudsters who cloak their extortions in the guise of magic. The current fashionability of spiritualist interpretations of mesmerism has, I fear, opened the door to a new generation of pretended magicians, and popularizations like Bulwer's will only serve to add further smoke to the sputtering fire.

"For two generations now, intelligent men have been struggling to determine whether or not there is any truth in the claims made by magnetizers, and, if so, what kind of truth it might be, but I fear that we are on the brink of a new era, in which any truth there might be will simply be drowned out by a deluge of impostures. The opportunities are simply too tempting: whatever else it is, or might become, magnetism provides a new theory of magic, which may be invoked to provide elegant explanations of past mysteries and license extravagant promises of future discovery and power. Saint-Germain was the first to see how vulnerable an organization like the Philosophical Harmonic Society might be to the influence of a clever poseur, but even he does not seem to have foreseen that his success in that regard would rapidly inspire admirers avid to seize his crown, as well as meek disciples content to bathe in his reflected glory.

"We are no longer living in the eighteenth century, my friend, let alone the seventeenth. The men who trumpeted the Age of Enlightenment were anticipating an end to the history of super-

stition, and a new era that would put paid to the idols of false belief that had tyrannized men in the past—but they underestimated the human hunger for belief in forces beyond nature and beyond reason. I do not say that Enlightenment will perish, but I do believe that it will find itself juxtaposed with a stubborn and increasingly sophisticated opposition. Mademoiselle Valdemar will certainly not be the last or best of her kind; indeed, I suspect that the next fifty years will see a positive plague of so-called mediums, who will wring every last drop out of the imaginative potential of magnetic sleep, and will only give up, if they ever do, when they have found some other quasi-magical theory and practice to replace it in justifying their relentless fakery as healers, clairvoyants and substitute saints."

"And so *ad infinitum?*" I suggested.

"I fear so, although I still feel free to hope not. I would be very sad indeed to think that the twentieth century will make no headway against the dire trend, and deeply depressed to discover that such follies were still thriving unabated in the twenty-first. Nevertheless, the hunger will remain, so long as we can find no better way to appease or nullify the appetite behind it. It will soothe my pride to play a part in nipping Mademoiselle Valdemar's fledgling career in the bug, since she has had the utter audacity to involve me in her scheme, but I am anxious that her inevitable downfall might involve a consequential risk of harm to a man I consider precious."

"Balzac, you mean?"

"I do. If Dupotet has been ensnared by Saint-Germain, that is a tragedy, but he is a hale fellow with all his wits about him, and must be accorded responsibility for his own self-defence. Balzac is a hypochondriac, who has ruined his health with massive doses of black coffee and quack medicines, and his titanic imagination and literary gifts only add to his psychological vulnerability. He was easy meat for a predator of Jana Valdemar's stripe. Like a spider that has trapped a fly, she has him half-digested already, and clearly believes that no one else can prevail against her persuasions—even me, let alone

Chapelain. In time, if left unchecked, she might easily be capable of ensnaring Victor Hugo himself."

"I must admit," I said, judiciously, "that I thought you had gone to the opposite extreme of diplomacy in your treatment of Balzac and Madame Hanska, by comparison with your earlier conduct in regard to Saint-Germain. I did wonder whether it might not have been kinder to tell them bluntly that they were the victims of a confidence trickster, and that there is no hope of any miracle cure in whatever Robert Collyer brought from London—if, indeed, he ever left London, or brought anything with him if he did."

"I am convinced that he did leave London, and that he did bring something with him, which he had every intention of delivering to you." Dupin told me. "I am equally convinced that he had no idea what it was, having not been properly fore-warned. Mademoiselle Valdemar is too scrupulous a planner to have left such gaps in her scheme. As I said before, her neo-Gothic melodrama has an aesthetic dimension as well as a criminal one. She is an artist, and a true one. To invade your house after contriving to drug you with the spice in your mulled wine, and to whisper the words: "Kiss me, my mortal lover!" in your ear, knowing exactly what images your dreaming mind would conjure up in response, is one thing; to repeat the performance by coming to my apartment—*mine!*—is something else entirely. That is not commonplace temerity but reckless genius. Whether she decided to involve me in her scheme because she feared that I might involve myself if she did not, or whether she simply wanted the challenge, I don't know, but in either case, an intelligence like that, coupled with a beautiful face, would be very easy to love—and perhaps very difficult to avoid loving. She must see herself as the ultimate *femme fatale*, and a worthy avatar of the Dweller of the Threshold. Poor fool that she is, in spite of all her intelligence!"

I thought that a bit rich, on more than one count. For one thing it seemed to me that invading my home and whispering in my ear while I slept was just as bold a move as repeating

the trick, given that Dupin and I were both mere mortals. For another, it seemed to me that he was showing an altogether unhealthy enthusiasm in complimenting his adversary, which contrasted strongly with the contempt he apparently felt for Saint-Germain. Even as a chivalrous concession to maidenhood, it seemed a trifle exaggerated—and I seriously doubted, in view of the company she kept, that Mademoiselle Valdemar could be reckoned a maiden, let alone a damsel in distress. It seemed more sensible, however, to make the attempt to bring Dupin back down to earth by talking about practical matters.

"Will we find Collyer, then, when we find Mademoiselle Valdemar?" I asked.

"Probably," Dupin replied. "I very much doubt that she has killed him—although the use of ether and other drugs designed to render men insensible is not without its risks."

A thought occurred to me. "But it is possible, is it not," I ventured, "that Collyer is her accomplice in this scheme—that he is the other man who was in my house this morning, and who drugged Saint-Germain?"

"Conceivable, but unlikely. If he were, it would introduce an ugly tuck, if not an actual gap, in her carefully-constructed story."

"Who is her accomplice, then?"

"I'm not certain—but I have a strong suspicion."

I did not press him; he would tell me when he was certain—or when he was ready, whichever was the sooner. There was, in any case, a more important question that needed settling before we reached our destination. We were outside the *enceinte* now, having passed through the *barrière* while he was in full flow, and I feared that our arrival might be imminent.

"What are you going to do when you confront her?" I asked. "How are you going to put a stop to her game?"

"To tell you the truth," he said, "although I have every reason to believe that her project will be comprehensively wrecked before the night is out, I'm not at all sure exactly what part I can or ought to play. I feel sorry for her, but I doubt that she will

allow me to save her, even if I try—which leaves me, I admit, in something of a quandary. I suppose I shall have to play it by ear."

"Oh," I said, more than a trifle disappointed by his peculiar attitude, and groping for a possible explanation of his querulousness. "You're worried, I suppose, that we might not be able to lift the spell that she has put on Balzac once you have thwarted her scheme?"

"That's certainly one thing that troubles me. It might be difficult to persuade Balzac that anyone but she can do the trick—although he does seem to trust me, and might have wisdom enough to guide his faith in that matter. We can, on the other hand, be quite certain that *she* can lift the curse that she has imposed on him, and if there is any way that she can still be allowed to do it…."

"She would probably refuse," I said, not liking the idea that his compassion might extend so far as to protect a wicked schemer, even for Balzac's sake.

"She certainly would not. Effecting a seeming cure of Balzac's illness is the crucial element of her plan. In spite of his literary success, he is not a rich man—we in France do not, alas, reward our men of genius as we ought, although we are no worse in that respect than any other nation in Europe, or the world. On the other hand, he *is* a famous man: a popular topic of discussion in every coffee-house, cabaret and estaminet in the city. If Mademoiselle Valdemar's luminous potion could work an apparent miracle on him, its apparent value would be assured, all the more so by virtue of the rumor being spread by means of clandestine whispers rather than the pages of the daily newspapers. The ultimate object of her cupidity is, inevitably, Saint-Germain—the Faubourg, not the impostor."

"If her scheme succeeds," I muttered, "she'll hardly be content with a mere Comte, especially a fake one—she'll have her eyes on a Duc."

"Perhaps," said Dupin. "Marriage—especially one made for money—would probably not inhibit her career as a seductress,

and might even lend it some assistance."

"Would her father be proud of her, do you think?" I wondered, aloud.

"An interesting question," Dupin observed. "Given that fathers have a tendency to be besotted with beautiful daughters, I suspect that he might—but one thing we must bear in mind is that there does not appear to have been any imposture on his part in all of this. Nathaniel Falconer and Andrew Davis might have exaggerated their accounts of the experiment, as might your correspondent, but the experiment *did* take place, and Valdemar *was* arrested on the brink of death for more than half a year. I can believe that the subject of such an experiment might have begun it with the intention of faking a trance, but it is beyond the bounds of credibility that anyone could have kept up any such fakery for seven months. I cannot tell whether he really did die during that interim, rather than at the moment of his apparent awakening, but in either case, I suspect that his invocation of the Dweller of the Threshold, although doubtless partly based on his reading of *Zanoni*, was quite spontaneous. That incident undoubtedly provided his daughter with the seed of her plan, but I cannot believe that she contrived it…unless, of course, she really does have supernatural powers."

"You surely don't believe that, Dupin?"

"I'm a good agnostic, my friend; I keep an open mind. You and I have both been witness to events that other men would unhesitatingly call supernatural, although you know full well that my own opinion is that our present definition of the natural is simply far too parsimonious to acknowledge them. That there are strange powers abroad in the world, I am perfectly prepared to admit—but that humans can possess them, I still beg leave to doubt. Perhaps Mademoiselle Valdemar can offer me some further insight into the possibility—but for now, I'm content to wonder, a trifle anxiously, whether *she* believes that she has supernatural powers, in addition to her manifest ingenuity in maintaining that image."

"Charlatans often fall victim to their own patter," I quoted.

"Exactly," he agreed.

"And the bigger the charlatans they are," I suggested, "the harder they're likely to fall?"

He did not bother to correct the awkwardness of my expression. He simply said: "I suspect so—and I pity her all the more because of it." Then he stopped, at the entrance to an unlit lane that led eastwards between two looming hedgerows.

Dupin attempted to consult his watch, and clicked his tongue in annoyance when he could not see the hands. The sun had long gone, and we were now surrounded by the dead of night, but it was not pitch dark. The moon was an unhelpful crescent, but the atmosphere was crisp and clear, and the stars shone brightly now that we had moved far enough away from the industrial smoke of regions clustered around the city's main arteries. In the distance, we could see a hamlet of cottages, grouped not far away from a house that might once have been a prosperous farmhouse—or, more likely, an impoverished manor. The grounds of the larger house were untidy and walls were overgrown with ivy, but its roof seemed to be in tolerably good repair, and its windows, gleaming in the starlight, intact.

"Do places like that have postal addresses now?" I asked.

"Most certainly," he said, as he put his watch away and stared at the crescent moon, as if hoping to deduce the time from its position relative to the zenith. "Organized postal services have not merely redefined human communities, but have revolutionized geography. From now on, every human dwelling will gradually acquire an address, even those in the dark heart of Africa and the wildernesses of the Far East. France has already succumbed in her entirety. Come on, my friend—we have an appointment with our tormentor. She has issued us a most ingenious invitation, and it would no more do to be late than too early…especially if we hope to save her from herself."

CHAPTER TEN
The Enchantress in Her Lair

Dupin made no attempt to approach the house stealthily, or to scout its surroundings before going in. He simply strolled up to the main door and rang the bell. It was not opened by a concierge or a valet, but by a tall man in a frock coat, who was carrying a gun in his fright hand, dangling it negligently by his side. I recognised it as a Colt revolver; although I had never handled one personally, I was familiar with its reputation as a key example of the industrial utility of the assembly line, and I studied it curiously. The oil-lamp in the vestibule was behind him, making it difficult to see his face, but Dupin looked the silhouette up and down appraisingly.

"Do you really believe that you will need the firearm, Dr. Falconer?" he asked, eventually.

"Your reputation as a logician is obviously not exaggerated, Monsieur Dupin," the tall man said, speaking in French but with a very distinct accent. "No, I'm assured that I won't need it—but I'm a true American, after all, and I don't like to be separated from my revolver." He glanced at me, as if to imply that I might not be a true American, given my long exile and my apparent unfamiliarity with Mr. Colt's invention, but he did not give me time to react before adding: "Anyway, I always reckon that one can't be too careful."

"Indeed not," said Dupin. "Is Mademoiselle Valdemar at home?"

"At home? That I doubt—she hardly stops complaining, in

spite of the trouble I've taken with the decorations. In temporary residence, certainly. She's been expecting you."

"I know. She promised me a kiss, but I was asleep at the time, and unable to comply with her request."

"Now, now," said the American, as he ushered us into the vestibule and closed the door behind us. "You mustn't try to make me jealous. She told me that you'd try to drive a wedge between us, operating on the principle of divide and rule. I'm wise to it. She anticipates everything—you have to admit that she's one hell of a pythoness."

"I'm sure that the serpentine analogy does her justice," Dupin remarked, slipping back into his silkiest tone—as he always did when preparing for verbal combat.

Nathaniel Falconer showed us into what must have been the dining-room n the days when the manor was in its heyday. I understood immediately what he had meant about the effort he had put into the décor. I had never been into the inner sanctums of the Harmonic Society, but I had always imagined them to be filled with relics stolen during Napoléon's Egyptian campaign and various items of neo-Pythagorean trumpery. There were no mummy-cases on display here, but there were variously-sized images of Bubastis and Sekhmet, some painted and others sculpted in sandstone, and there were diagrams of the zodiac too, mounted on screens. Pride of place on the open space above the huge slate fireplace was given, as on the Great Seal of the United States, to a depiction of the All-Seeing Eye. There was, however, a brass-framed clock on the mantelpiece, whose evident modernity struck a slightly jarring note. Having been forewarned, I took note of the glance that Dupin directed at it, and his apparent satisfaction with the position of the hands.

The large bay window set in the wall opposite the room's double-battened main door was curtained off by heavy red velvet drapes, but we had entered by a lateral door, so the curtains were to our left as we faced the throne on which Mademoiselle Valdemar was seated. Actually, it was merely a wooden armchair embellished in supposed imitation of a throne,

but it was set on a shallow podium in order that she might look down even on tall men like Falconer and Dupin. Although she was not made up in the image of Cleopatra or Nefertiti, there was something Pharaonic in the styling of her black hair, and the kohl with which she had made up her startling eyes. Her lips were carefully carmined. She was probably thirty, but she had an aura of youth as well as a suggestion of magical authority.

"I've been expecting you, Messieurs," she said, in a husky voice designed fr seduction. "Thank you for coming."

"If you expect to persuade anyone that I came to deliver Collyer's package," I said, impulsively, "I shall deny it."

"Of course you will," she replied, "but there are intrigues of a sort in which every denial is construed as an admission, and vice versa. The rumor is already flying through the heart of Paris—no small thanks to you—and it only remains for me to reap my reward. Fiction, if adequately crafted, is so much more powerful than truth, simply by virtue of being specifically and artfully designed to appeal to the imagination."

"Is Dr. Collyer here?" Dupin asked, mildly.

"Upstairs," Jana Valdemar confirmed. "Asleep and confused, but quite well. He will wake up to find his parcel gone—but he will be reassured when he discovers that it has reached its rightful owner. The kindest thing to do would be to let him believe that you recovered it, and saved him too, before dutifully completing your part of the mission—but that is your choice to make."

"We're not the only ones who'll tell a different story," I put in.

"Perhaps not, if you decide to do that," she said, "but you might not be able to rely on overmuch support. The Comte will decide, in the end, that there's more profit in being with me than against me—and I think my powers of persuasion will be equal to keeping Dupotet and Chapelain silent, even if they're reluctant to endorse my claims. Balzac and his mistress I hold in the palm of my hand."

"Your trump cards, so to speak," Dupin put in.

"So to speak," she agreed.

"And Dr. Falconer does not mind sharing you with so many other lovers, I suppose?" Dupin said, darting a sly sideways glance at the man with the revolver. "You've doubtless told him that he is the foremost among them—the special one—just as you've doubtless assured him that he will get his full share of your gains, in spite of the urgent demands of your noble political cause…assuming that to be the current disguise you've adopted for your avarice."

She had expected that line of attack, and looked lazily in Falconer's direction, as if to say: "I told you so." To Dupin, she simply said: "You mustn't be jealous, Monsieur Dupin. You should take it as a compliment that I approached you on an intellectual level."

"By stealing into my apartment and whispering: 'Kiss me, my mortal lover!' into my ear as I slept?"

"That was only a tiny part of my scheme," she pointed out, "and not a vital one. Again, you mustn't be jealous, simply because I did as much for your loyal friend—who had the decency to try to wake up in response, although he could not quite achieve it."

"Might I see your supposed elixir of life, Mademoiselle?" Dupin asked, politely.

"You may see it, Monsieur Dupin," Jana Valdemar replied, with a feline smile, "but you mustn't touch. It's a very valuable substance now." She stressed the word *now* very faintly.

She had obviously anticipated the request, for she had the metal cylinder ready behind her mock-throne. She bought it out and unscrewed the cap, then tilted the neck of the container towards us so that we could see the faintly-gleaming substance within—but then she withdrew the canister and clutched it to her bosom, almost as if it were her first-born child.

"How fortunate we are to live in an era of chemical miracles!" she said. "New substances are being discovered all the while, with all kinds of strange properties. One day, all our streets will be lit so brightly that night will be entirely banished."

Dupin did not attempt to take the slightest step forward in pursuit of the cylinder. "But that is nature's artifice, is it not?" he said, mildly. "You are an artist, after all, and no mere conjuror. That really is your father's mortal remains, if my guess is right—or a part of them?"

"It's all there," Falconer put in, as he leaned negligently on the jamb of the double-battened door to our right. "All that's left of it, at any rate. You have no idea how difficult it was to claim the whole residue, when Davis was so very keen to continue his own experiments, but I had to do it, once I received Jana's letter. As you say, Mr. Dupin, she's an artist. She likes to do things properly—and so do I. You needn't worry, though—the cylinder and its contents have been very thoroughly sterilized, and Davis did enough to prove that they aren't toxic…not to dogs, at any rate. We'll be working with very low doses, at any rate—in full accordance with the Hippocratic principle of doing no harm. We'll be dispensing suggestions of well-being, after all, not promises of immortality. We might well content ourselves with anointing foreheads rather than tongues, to make absolutely certain that we only communicate the right contagion."

"If only it were that simple," said Dupin, mournfully. Then he paused.

Jana Valdemar knew that the pause was calculated for dramatic effect, and that she was about to face some kind of subtle attack, but she only smiled. She had no lack of self-confidence, and she felt quite at home in her surroundings, no matter how much complaining she had done while Falconer was dressing the set.

"It *is* that simple, Monsieur Dupin," she said. "I know that it must have seemed complicated to you, while you worked your way through the maze, but it always was quite simple. As Nat says, we won't be poisoning anyone."

"Probably not," Dupin conceded. "Except of course, yourselves."

Falconer actually laughed at that. "Don't worry, Mr. Dupin,"

he said. "We shan't be tempted to overdose on our own medicine, in the hope that we might become immortal. We know better than that."

"If the account that Chapelain gave us was reliable," Dupin retorted, his voice still as mild as milk, but his eyes as sharp as daggers as they directed another rapid glance at the clock, "you did not know enough to interpret Monsieur Valdemar's vision correctly. As my friend pointed out to Chapelain, the idea that your father's metamorphosis might have produced an elixir of life does not seem to make sense, on a superficial level."

"But our analysis is not superficial," Mademoiselle Valdemar put in. "Our contention is that my father was already dead—as he had to be—when his vision of the Dweller of the Threshold gave him access to occult knowledge that he could only have obtained while in that curious posthumous sleep-state. He could not bring himself back to life by means of the metamorphosis he learned to effect, but he could and did transform his mortal remains into a substance that might help his fellow men, like the great and selfless scholar he was."

"But that's not what really happened, Mademoiselle Valdemar," Dupin said, almost casually.

"You can have no idea what really happened, Monsieur Dupin, as you were not there—and you know full well that the only thing that matters is what people believe to have happened. We have an eye-witness, and we have the substance itself. Our account is the one that will be believed, no matter how many logicians oppose us, or how clever they are."

"The fact remains, Mademoiselle Valdemar, that you and Falconer have misinterpreted the situation—and, as a matter of fact, I *do* know what really happened, even though I was not there."

Few people in the world could have resisted the temptation, in such circumstances, to say: "How?" Jana Valdemar was not one of the exceptions.

"I had a dream," Dupin told her. "Due, I admit, in no small part, to you—but you were not to know that the words you

spoke would not awaken the same associations in my mind as they did in my friend's."

"Are you saying that you have not read *Zanoni?*" she asked.

"More attentively than you, it seems—and with a better sense of discrimination. I had met the Dwellers of the Thresholds before, you see. I am acquainted with more than one of them. I do not say that I am on good terms with them, or even that they deign to reckon me a rival—but I do understand them a little better than any mere reader of Bulwer's earnest fantasy, and I know what that potion can and will do, if it is used indiscriminately."

I had, of course, been somewhat forewarned of the kind of attack that Dupin might mount on the woman who had tricked him into playing a bit part in her bold charade. Charlatans, he had told me twice over, are ever wont to fall victim to their own lines of patter. If it is difficult for ordinary individuals to resist the stubborn hunger for supernatural explanation to which he had earlier referred, how much harder is it for those who pose as magicians? The very success of their impostures is perennially apt to lead their satisfaction beyond the bounds of reason.

Mademoiselle Valdemar was however, younger than the self-styled Comte de Saint-Germain and less experienced, doubly armored by her naïve cynicism and the fact that she had not yet grown excessively used to wielding the power that she sought. I was by no means sure that she would fall for the ploy. She was still smiling as she said: "I knew that you would not let me down, Monsieur Dupin. I prepared myself for surprises, and you have not failed me. You are an adept, then, in spite of your professed rationalism? You really are what the Comte and I claim to be—but you, respectful of the demands of your status, have kept it strictly secret until now, even from your closest friend." She glanced at me with a kind of amused contempt that I did not like at all.

"No, Mademoiselle Valdemar, I make no claim to be an adept," Dupin countered. "I am not what you pretend to be, but what your friend with the revolver pretends to be: an objec-

tive researcher, interested in sorting out the intellectual wheat from the chaff wherever strange phenomena are manifest. I am a voracious reader, though not a credulous one, and I have been fortunate enough, in the course of my empirical enquiries, to encounter more than my fair share of events and entities that surpass present-day human understanding, on which the produce of my reading might be brought to bear."

"Including the Dweller of the Threshold?" the lady queried, sarcastically.

"Bulwer slipped into the singular too," Dupin observed, "when describing Glyndon's misadventure—but when Mejnour introduced the term to the narrative, he spoke in the plural, at least with respect to the first term. His initial assertion was that there is a whole world of living beings—or beings that share some of the attributes of life—within the connective interstices between worlds, just as there is in the microcosm within a drop of water, or within an atom, or in the worlds akin to our own that lie alongside it, displaced in other spatial dimensions, or in the macrocosm of which our entire universe is but an atom, or a fraction of an atom. Like Leibniz, you see, Mejnour is a diehard plenarist—a man who thinks the very notion of empty space inconceivable, a benevolent illusion of our senses that allows us to exist in a false simplicity rather than a complexity with which our primitive intelligence could not cope."

"But still," the lady said, a trifle impatiently, "setting aside all the high-flown bluster, you affirm that you had met the Dwellers of the Thresholds—including the one cited by Bulwer, who says: 'Kiss me, my mortal lover!'—before the novel was even written?"

"Yes."

"And did you kiss the one with the terrible eyes?"

"No—but unlike you, I believe that your father might really have done so."

"In a dream!"

"In a vision experienced while in state of magnetic sleep, by a man who might have been dead already, or in some state of

uncertainty for which we have no name, intermediate between life and death. Are you, or Dr. Falconer, prepared to assert that there is no truth at all in the claims made by mesmerists regarding magnetic sleep, or the experiences sometimes undergone therein by somniloquists?"

Mademoiselle Valdemar might, I think, have been ready to issue exactly that assertion, on the basis of her own experience as an accomplished faker, and judging others by herself—but Falconer the mesmerist was not sure. "I *was* there, Mr. Dupin," he said flipping his gun from his right hand to his left and back again, "and I'm willing to conceded that what Valdemar experienced, when Davis and I invited him to make use of his inner vision, was something other than an ordinary dream, such as a sleeping man might experience—but the report I gave Chapelain was honest enough, and I'm fully convinced that the images that came into his head, fabricated in response to our prompts, were dredged up from his memory of reading *Zanoni*. That is the simple explanation—why should we search for any other, let alone one that is as implausible as it is exotic?"

"Because," said Dupin, firmly, "even if you are right, we must entertain the hypothesis that Monsieur Valdemar had read *Zanoni* more attentively than you appear have done, and that his metamorphosis was no mere matter of producing a benevolent panacea."

"Go on, Monsieur Dupin," said Jana Valdemar, still interested to hear what he had to say, in spite of the fact that she was determined not to believe a word of it.

"According to what Mejnour told Glyndon," Dupin went on, "the elixir of life that he desired so avidly was a two-edged sword, whose promise was a seductive trap. To anyone not elaborately prepared to receive its gift—specifically, prepared to be capable of withstanding the hostile depredations of the Dwellers of the Thresholds—it would not bring life but horror and doom. And that, I fear, is what it brought to your father, who was by no means prepared for the deadly kiss he recklessly imparted. That much is obvious even in Poe's abridged account—and it

was doubly obvious to me when the suggestion you whispered in my ear opened my own mind, very briefly, to the perception of the Dwellers."

"When the Dweller with the Eyes of Fire demanded a kiss of you, which you refused?"

"No, Mademoiselle Valdemar," Dupin countered, his voice suddenly becoming firm and harsh. "When I saw the Dweller with the Eyes of Fire demanding the obscene kiss from you—*which you no longer had any alternative but to accept!*"

CHAPTER ELEVEN
The Dweller with the Eyes of Fire

The ploy failed—or so it seemed to me. Jana Valdemar did not flinch, but laughed instead. Her laughter was exceptionally musical: an altogether natural element of her uncanny seductiveness.

"Am I possessed, then?" she demanded. "Have I given my soul to the Dwellers, without even knowing it, and sealed my doom?"

"I fear so," said Dupin, sorrowfully. "And I fear, too, that the realization will not be long delayed—but it might not be too late, if you will consent to hear me now, and do as I advise." As he pronounced the words *too late* he glanced at the clock again, carefully measuring the time that was passing as the strange scene unfolded.

"Of course," the lady replied, still laughing, apparently enjoying the contest of wits. "You intend to cite Pierre's beloved principle of contagion, which he could not refrain from adding into our story. That is the way that legends grow, you know—as each teller passes the story alone, he adds a small embellishment of his own. According to you, then, my father's remains, far from having a curative value, operate as a subtle poison, not by way of ingestion—for they are not toxic in any vulgar sense, albeit a trifle odorous—but by way of a mysterious contagion that affects those who maintain contact with their container for any length of time. Poor Nat has been doomed for some time, then, for he had them in his custody throughout their Atlantic

crossing, albeit in his trunk, safely stowed in the hold—but I am beginning to catch him up now…unless I repent my wicked ways immediately, hand over the elixir to your virtuous safe keeping, and go into a nunnery? Is that your story, Monsieur Dupin? Does your down-to-earth friend find *that* plausible?"

She looked at me; it was a challenge. "If that is what my friend contends," I replied, stoutly, "then I believe it." I did not believe a word of it, of course, but I did not think the heroic lie unduly transparent.

"I saw the Dweller with the Eyes of Fire exact her kiss from you, Mademoiselle," Dupin said, equably. "Yes, I was dreaming, but sometimes, even in dreams—perhaps especially in dreams—the cracks in the universe open up to our perception. The plenarists are right, of course; there is no empty space. What we presently believe to be void is, in fact, full of matter that our meager senses cannot apprehend: multiple universes stacked within one another and alongside one another, *ad infinitum*—or nearly so. For the most part, I must suppose, those other universes, placed within our reach but not within our grasp, are inhabited by beings whose own senses leave them utterly oblivious to all the other universes except their own—but in a near-infinite universe, all things are possible. Sometimes, thresholds open up in the interstices between the universes, which may serve as portals enabling the passage of information, energy, or even matter, between them, and those thresholds have their dwellers—who are, for the most part, predators lying in ambush. They do not aliment themselves on flesh, but on souls. In order to do that, they may induce metamorphoses in the flesh, which make souls more digestible. You asked me whether you should repent your wicked ways immediately—to which my answer is yes, and would be yes, whatever the circumstances. You also asked me whether you should hand over the elixir for my virtuous sake-keeping, to which my answer is also yes—but instead of asking me that silly question as to whether you should go into a nunnery, you should have asked me the most important question of all, which is more urgent than you

seem to suspect."

Again, he paused. His showmanship was a trifle crude, to tell the truth, but he had assistance now. The lamps in the old dining-room, which had never burned particularly bright, were burning much lower now than when we had started our little drama, and there was a draught from the bay that was causing the flames to flicker somewhat, casting strange reflections around the room. The variously-sized statues of Bubastis and Sekhmet were projecting predatory shadows, and the images on the screens were afflicted by odd nuances. The red velvet curtains were actually moving, as if their folds were indolent waves on a breeze-lapped sea.

Jana Valdemar was sitting very still, but the stillness was bought by tension as she fought to control herself. She was, however, a consummate confidence-trickster, and was determined not to be tricked herself.

"I like you, Monsieur Dupin," she said. "I wish you were a mesmerist, eager to experiment with my somniloquistic powers. You have no idea how easy it is to seduce mesmerists—literally as well as metaphorically—by playing the innocent sleeper. Those who pose as objective men of science are easiest of all—ask your friends Dupotet and Chapelain, if dear Nat is not evidence enough for you. If only you really were an adept… or thought you were…but I shall not give up hope just yet. Just look into my eyes when you tell me what the most important question of all might be—and then look at my blood-red lips, and imagine them saying to you: 'Kiss me, my mortal lover!'"

She was good, but Dupin was better. "The question you should have asked me, my poor, dear Mademoiselle Valdemar," he said, with what I took to be a contrived sigh of compassion, and speaking with a metronomic regularity, "is whether my vision of the Dweller with the Eyes of Fire coming to claim her kiss, and your soul along with it, was a vision of the past, the present, or the future—because the answer, my poor, lovely pythoness, is that it was a vision of the future. *And that future was now!*"

I did not have time to wonder whether Dupin had let his pedantic standards slip for once, because the moment he had pronounced the word *now* he leapt to his left, and took firm hold of the red velvet curtains, and ripped them down. The rod supporting them did not appear to be rotten, but he must have given it a strong tug, and Falconer evidently had not had the time or the patience to screw them securely to the wall. They billowed as they fell, but they fell abruptly, and Dupin ducked as they fell, as if in order to avoid looking through the window.

Everyone else, of course, looked at the panes and the night behind them.

And beyond the window thus exposed burned two enormous eyes of fire, avid with fury.

I would swear on all I hold sacred that my heart actually stopped—although it started again after missing a single beat.

The interval between my interrupted heartbeats could not have been more than a fraction of a second, in real time—but it seemed to me that a gap opened up in time within that margin, and that my soul, if not my physical senses, somehow contrived to adapt to the absence, so that my mind's inner eye continued to see.

What I saw, while time was suspended, was that the space between myself and the night beyond the window was not empty at all, and that the invisible molecules of air that I knew to be filling it were crowded in their distant isolation by millions upon millions of entire universes, packed so closely that the interfaces between them were devoid of space...but not, in some strange sense, devoid of substance. My soul saw, although my eyes could not, that, as well as the countless components of the multiverse, there were creatures living in between them, lying in ambush outside spaces and times, waiting for opportunities to reach within one universe or another, as fishermen reach into the liquid element. There were as many creatures as universes, and perhaps more, of all kinds of shapes and dimensions—but there was one out of all those Dwellers of the Thresholds that was lying in ambush for *us*...or, at least, for one of our number.

As the sphinx-like Dweller with the Eyes of Fire pounced, it seemed to my admittedly-confused vision that she passed through a million universes in the course of her leap, although I doubt that the inhabitants of any of them perceived her passage—and it was only in seeing the extent and effort of that leap that I was able to realize the true magnitude of her hunger, and the true perversity of her appetite.

Such was the distortion of my conceptual geometry that she seemed to be leaping directly at me, although I was not her objective, and I knew when she spoke the fated words—"Kiss me, my mortal lover!"—that they were not, on this occasion, addressed to me.

I did not even have to refuse, and was very glad of that, for I had no dream-insulation about me then, and if the invitation had been addressed to me, I am not at all sure that I would have been able to resist.

In brief, although I could not help experiencing the vision—in spite of the fact that I had adequate forewarning of the kind of trick that Dupin intended to work, and the fact that I have never considered myself an unusually suggestible person—I got off lightly.

Jana Valdemar's stiff resistance had already turned brittle, and it simply shattered. I have never heard a scream as intense as the one she emitted as she leapt to her feet, horror-struck. In *her* mind's eye, she received the Dweller's assault full on. As befit the accomplished seductress she was, her kiss was ready and willing, but she knew even as she offered it that it was a calamitous and self-destructive act. My mind's eye saw more than any common eye was capable of seeing, and saw the terror evoked by her consciousness of her doom. The vision was literally indescribable, so you will simply have to believe me when I say that the mere awareness of it cut through me like a dagger, hurting me agonizingly, even though it inflicted no lasting wound.

I cannot pretend that I actually saw Mademoiselle Valdemar's soul being devoured, even in my mind's magical eye, but I do

affirm that I felt the most horrid pang of sympathy and pity that ever afflicted me in the whole of my life—and I understood, then, why Dupin had felt sorry for the victim of the illusion he had set out to manufacture.

Nathaniel Falconer did not scream—but he made plenty of noise as he raised his revolver and started firing, fanning the hammer of the weapon with his free hand as the squeezed the trigger again and again. He must have released all six bullets within the space of five seconds, under conditions that did not permit him to take aim; the bullets went anywhere and everywhere, the whining of the ricochets mingling with the staccato echoes of the shots. It was a wonder that they found no human target—nor any supernatural one, of course.

Dupin, as a chivalrous man, had no hesitation in diving back toward the ersatz throne, seizing hold of Jana Valdemar's body and dragging her down to the floor, where he made every effort to cover her slender body with his own. I presume, however, that as no random bullet struck him, none would have struck her either.

For my part, once my heart was beating again, I tried to grab the smallest of the sandstone statues and hurl it at Falconer's head. Had my muscles been able to answer the demands of my feverish brain, it would have knocked him over before he fired the fifth shot, let alone the sixth, but it was a very heavy statue. I did, with enormous effort, contrive to throw it, but its movement through the air was painfully slow, and it fell short. It did knock him over, eventually, but only by rebounding into his shins. He howled in agony, though, in a very satisfactory manner, and showed no sign of getting to his feet again. The gun spun away into a corner of the room.

The illusion lasted no longer than half the time it took Falconer to fire the shots, but that was far too long for Jana Valdemar, who had shut her seductive eyes before then, and still had them shut as she lay on the ground in a fetal position, squeaking like a mouse.

I, however, was still standing up, and was able then to see

that the eyes of fire still floating beyond the bay window were, in fact, painted Chinese lanterns, whose seeming hostility was mere hasty artifice.

Several of the window-panes had been shattered by flying fragments of lead, but there were still enough remaining for the casement to need careful opening, in order to allow a well-dressed man to step through.

I was extremely surprised to see him. So was Dupin.

"Oh, come on!" said the self-styled Comte de Saint-Germain to his rival. "You don't really think that *mouches* are honest and reliable, because they work for the police? You shouldn't have set him to follow me when I left your friend's house if you did not want him corrupted. In any case, I did a far better job of collaborating with your little hoax than Dupotet and Chapelain would have done, had they even deigned to answer your call for help. Didn't I do a first-rate job with the lanterns? Wasn't my timing impeccable, in spite of the tight margin you gave me? Nor do I intend to drive a hard bargain now, for I freely admit that this was a joint effort, in which I could not have succeeded half so well without you. Even so, I must demand that you surrender the girl to me. She'll be a tremendous asset to me now she's learned her limitations, once she's got it into her delicate little skull that her soul hasn't actually been torn apart and devoured. You can have Collyer, and the fake elixir—I wouldn't dirty my hands with it now, and you're probably the only one who can stand in for Jana at Balzac's bedside. I certainly wouldn't want the second greatest writer in France to suffer as a result of this silly charade. I'll take Falconer too, as a makeweight to balance the deal. He's a natural candidate for the Harmonic Society, in any case. Agreed?"

Dupin hesitated, seemingly still frustrated by the fact that, although his intricately-timed plan had worked, it had been completed by the wrong collaborator. Eventually, he said: "Why should I let you take anything?"

"Because you're an honest man, if for no other reason," the ersatz Comte said, with some slight asperity. "I can't imagine

that you need, or really want, anything more than I'm offering you, but for what it's worth, I didn't come alone—and we'll be doing you a favor by taking these two off your hands, at least in the short term. You've got other fish to fry."

Dupin refused to say anything, but he bent down to pick up the cylinder in which the supposed elixir of life was contained, and turned to me. "Collyer's upstairs," he muttered. "We'd best check that he's all right. By the time we can wake him up and get him downstairs, all of this will probably have been cleared away."

He was right.

CHAPTER TWELVE
Saving Monsieur Balzac

We called in at my home before setting off for Balzac's house, in order to tidy ourselves up and collect a few necessities. Although he was no dandy, Dupin was a man who cared about his appearance, and so was I.

"Do you know, Dupin," I said, as we left the house again and made our way to the cab-stand on the boulevard, "even though I knew vaguely what to expect, your suggestion worked as powerfully on me as it must have done on Mademoiselle Valdemar. I mean, there was a sense in which I really did *see* the Dwellers of the Thresholds in my imagination, as clearly as I ever saw anything by means of my eyes. The mind can play strange tricks, with the right prompting. I don't mind admitting that it was almost enough to shake my steadfast faith in the fabric of reality. Were I an innocent in such matters, it might easily have seemed to be a true revelation—an authentic Road to Damascus moment, albeit of a Satanic rather than a divine variety. Mercifully, it's not the first time that you and I have confronted such illusions. If our acquaintance continues, I dare say that I'll eventually become an old hand, inured to any sort of psychic shock."

"You're a lucky man, my friend," Dupin replied, as we climbed into the fiacre.

I probably blushed slightly. "Well," I said, as we moved off, "I'm not there yet, I admit. I suppose I'm lucky that my heart consented to start again, once it had stopped—but even

Mademoiselle Valdemar wasn't actually struck dead. Not permanently, at any rate. I suppose, in a way, I really was dead for that fraction of a second, suspended between heartbeats. We think of life as something continuous and uninterrupted—even consciousness survives in sleep, although in an altered state—but there's a sense, isn't there, in which even time isn't really continuous?"

I paused briefly, and the rattle of the cab's wheels over the cobbles of the *quai* seemed to be trying to illustrate my point. "Although we perceive our existence as seamless," I went on, thoughtfully, "we die over and over again, perhaps a thousand or a million times a day, but are enabled by the constitution of our bodies and minds to return from those deaths, while circumstances remain normal. Circumstances can be varied, though, by virtue of natural or contrived effects, and when they become abnormal...well, strange things may occur. Poor Valdemar couldn't get back to normality, could he? And just for a moment, out there, I might not have been able to get back either. Thank God for my sound and stubborn heart!"

"Amen to that," said Dupin, softly.

When we had arrived and I had paid the coachman, Madame Hanska took us straight up to Balzac's bedroom. The great man seemed to be in a parlous state, but he perked up on seeing us come in.

"You have news?" he croaked.

Dupin knelt down beside the bed. "Yes indeed, Maître," he said. "Dr. Collyer has been found, and the elixir recovered. Mademoiselle Valdemar has been injured, I fear, and will take some time to make a full recovery, but she entrusted the elixir to me, because I am aware of its dangers as well as its virtues. I must ask you, though, never to speak of this to anyone. I will not be so vulgar as to ask a price for your treatment, but you are a worthy and imaginative man, and I know that you are fully aware of the consequences that might stem from reckless adver-tisement. I must implore you never to breathe a word of what has

happened in the course of this sad affair—and I feel obliged to warn you that what has befallen Mademoiselle Valdemar, whom you will not be seeing again, might yet befall others. We are dealing here with forces that are beyond human understanding and control, although I am sufficiently competent in their use to deploy them to your advantage."

"My lips are sealed," Balzac whispered. Privately, I hoped that they would stay sealed, if ever he had the misfortune to encounter the Dweller with the Eyes of Fire again.

"Mine too," Madame Hanska promised.

"It is important that you understand, Monsieur Balzac," Dupin continued, "That I cannot work miracles. I can cure much of what ails you at present, and perhaps the greater part of what ails you in general, but I cannot turn back the clock. You are no longer a young man, and you have used your flesh more harshly than you might have done, in the interests of your work. I cannot regret that bargain any more than you do, but I cannot unseal it either. I cannot grant you eternal life, or perpetual freedom from the pains of the flesh. All I can do is save you from imminent death, and grant you a margin of opportunity in which to continue your great project."

"I'll take what I can get," Balzac whispered, "and will be grateful to you, Monsieur Dupin. I shall not hold it against you that you cannot make me young again—for that might take away my wisdom, if not my inspiration."

"That's a wise reply," Dupin told him. "I shall show you the elixir now, so that you might judge its glow—and then I shall give you something to drink, which you must consume in its entirety."

I have noticed, in the course of my own experience, that if you make two statements in succession, their hearer will naturally assume a connection between them, even when there is none. Good logicians are ever alert for the potential error, but even the greatest logician might be forgiven an oversight when he believes himself to be on his deathbed.

Dupin opened the canister that he had appropriated from

Jana Valdemar, so that Balzac and Madame Hanska could see what was within it. He did not tell them that the luminosity was the stuff of haloes, but allowed them to draw their own conclusions. Then he gave Balzac a flask, made of the same alloy as the cylinder, from which to drink.

"It tastes like mulled wine," Balzac observed. There was a good reason for that. After a pause, the great man added: "But there is something unusual about the spices—an unfamiliar ingredient."

"Indeed there is," Dupin agreed. "Indeed there is."

When Balzac had fallen asleep, Dupin asked me to take Madame Hanska downstairs, and I obeyed. For that reason, I never got to hear what it was that he whispered into Balzac's ear, and was unable to measure the exact extent of the suggestion that he offered. I could not, in any case, have known what dreams might have been provoked in Balzac's mind by the prompt, although I very much doubt that they derived from the pages of *Zanoni*.

"He is saved, then?" Madame Hanska asked me, anxiously, while we waited for Duping to come down again.

"For the time being," I said. "You should try to limit his intake of coffee, though. I do not know of any man who ever poisoned himself by that means, but anything can be fatal if the dose is large enough." *Even credulity*, I added, silently.

"He will not take any action that inhibits his work," she replied. "How could anyone ask him to, given what he is? I love him, but...."

"I understand," I said. "We all do what we can, for those we love, but there are moral as well as physical limits to human contrivance."

Dupin was subdued when he came down again, and he remained so during the journey home.

As we passed over the Pont de la Raison to gain the Île de la Cité, Dupin leaned out of the *portière* and hurled the canister containing the elixir of life into the Seine, where it made a dull splash and immediately sank. I could see that the gesture cost

him dear; he was an ardent collector, after all, and an elixir of life, however false or dangerous, makes an interesting addition to any cabinet of curiosities.

"Was that necessary?" I queried. "Was it even wise?"

"I don't know," he confessed. "I am not one of those excessively humble souls who believe that there are things that humans are not meant to know, but nor do I have sufficient faith in my own good character, or anyone else's, to believe that humans are ready, as yet, to confront and repel the Dwellers of the Thresholds."

I loved him very dearly, and had all the respect in the world for his intellect, but sometimes I wondered if even he might be the kind of expert performer who is ever likely to fall victim to his own line of patter.

ABOUT THE AUTHOR

Brian Stableford was born in Yorkshire in 1948. He taught at the University of Reading for several years, but is now a full-time writer. He has written many science-fiction and fantasy novels, including *The Empire of Fear, The Werewolves of London, Year Zero, The Curse of the Coral Bride, The Stones of Camelot*, and *Prelude to Eternity*. Collections of his short stories include a long series of *Tales of the Biotech Revolution*, and such idiosyncratic items as *Sheena and Other Gothic Tales* and *The Innsmouth Heritage and Other Sequels*. He has written numerous nonfiction books, including *Scientific Romance in Britain, 1890-1950*; *Glorious Perversity: The Decline and Fall of Literary Decadence*; *Science Fact and Science Fiction: An Encyclopedia*; and *The Devil's Party: A Brief History of Satanic Abuse*. He has contributed hundreds of biographical and critical articles to reference books, and has also translated numerous novels from the French language, including books by Paul Féval, Albert Robida, Maurice Renard, and J. H. Rosny the Elder.